PRUDENCE CRANDALL

PRUDENCE CRANDALL

Woman of Courage

ELIZABETH YATES

BOYDS MILLS PRESS

Published by Caroline House
Boyds Mills Press, Inc.
A Highlights Company
815 Church Street
Honesdale, Pennsylvania 18431
Printed in the United States of America

Publisher Cataloging-in-Publication Data
Yates, Elizabeth.
Prudence Crandall : Woman of courage / by Elizabeth Yates.—2nd ed.
[144]p. : cm.
Originally published by E.P. Dutton Co, N.Y., 1955.
Summary : A new edition of the historical novel of the Quaker teacher who in 1833 opened a school for African-American women and girls.
ISBN 1-56397-391-X
1. Crandall, Prudence, 1803-1890—Juvenile Literature. 2. Afro-Americans—Education—Connecticut—Juvenile Literature. 3. Canterbury (Conn.)—History—Juvenile Literature. 4. Abolitionists—United States—Juvenile Literature.
[1. Crandall, Prudence, 1803-1890. 2. Afro-Americans—Education—Connecticut. 3. Canterbury (Conn.)—History. 4. Abolitionists—United States—Biography.]
371.1 / 0092 / 4—dc20 [B] 1996
Library of Congress Catalog Card Number 93-74857

First Boyds Mills Press edition, 1996
The text of this book is set in 11-point Palatino
Portrait of Prudence Crandall reproduced by permission of the Division of Rare and Manuscript Collections, Carl A. Kroch Library, Cornell University, Ithaca, New York.

10 9 8 7 6 5 4 3 2 1

To

HOWARD THURMAN—courageous teacher
who kindles minds and strengthens hearts

Contents

Prudence Crandall
Portrait courtesy of Cornell University

INTRODUCTION

There is so much to say about this fine book, one scarcely knows where to begin. Certainly the very first comment to make on the exciting story is to note the way it keeps a reader turning over the pages to see what can have happened next. A made-up, invented tale, no matter how skillful the author, can never have the strong, urgent, actual suspense-interest of events known to have really happened. Imagine how thin the story of Paul Revere's famous ride would be, if it were just an imaginary adventure story, a piece of fiction, even ever so cleverly written a piece of fiction. American hearts beat faster as they watch Paul Revere climb into the saddle for the ride which, for all he knew, might end in his violent death. What stirs our blood is the fact that a real flesh-and-blood human being, a living patriot actually did thus risk his life for a cause very dear to us.

The story of the young Prudence Crandall's stout-hearted resistance to danger and violence inspirits us in the same way. There really was a patriotic Prudence Crandall who fought bravely against heavy odds for what we now love as one of the bases of our American heritage. She is no imaginary heroine. She was a slender young woman, with bright blue eyes, soft blond hair, and a special way of speaking, quiet, controlled, "lady-like," as people said in the early part of the 1800's,—but firm as granite. The author of this book has searched letters, memoirs, documents of all kinds, and has found out so much about her, that we can actually see her as she stood, brave as a lion, in her decorous, long, spreading skirts, her well-brushed golden hair gleaming, her bonnet-strings tied neatly under her firm chin.

And how we can see and hear the uproar of violence that battered against the fine old house in the fine old Connecticut village. It was a battlefield, on which Prudence Crandall stood under fire, her sweet young sister beside her, on the front line of a struggle then just beginning, which was soon to spread all over our nation. Long after the reader has finished the book, his ears ring with the clamor of the astonishing attacks made on that brave pioneer woman, not by yelling Indians, circling around unarmed women in a lonely frontier homestead, but by raging mass prejudice, in what was, outwardly, one of the most peaceful and stable backgrounds in American history. It would be incredible, if it were not as true as true, on record, each step of the to-and-fro swaying of the conflict set down in reliable and often official documents.

The old American who writes this introduction has firm hope and faith in our younger generation and hence is rejoiced to see a powerful story, powerfully told, put into the hands of our young people—and of their parents, to most of whom this extraordinary chronicle will be entirely new. American youth, old enough to read this narrative of magnificent bravery, are not far from the age when on them will be laid the tremendous moral responsibility of being citizens and defenders of a democracy. They need to be prepared for this responsibility by anything which can be learned from our history. We try to safeguard their personal lives as grown-ups by giving them in advance some ideas of what physical and moral dangers will threaten their integrity. Many of the stories written for them describe how other people before them have bravely and persistently resisted such dangers. But the collective life of human communities also is threatened by special dangers, as much as individual life, and, to resist them, courage and determination of a special kind are as much needed as in personal trials. Examples of such courage can be inspiringly drawn from our past history,—such as are in this story of Prudence Crandall.

Could anything be more heart-shaking and strength-giving than the wonderful, factually, literally true incident (which ends this book) of public group-confession of error for a terrible mistake, collectively made; of remorse by a human community for the wrongs by their group done in earlier years. Could you find anywhere a darker, more desparate tale of communal wrong-doing, followed by a more open-hearted, open-handed effort to make amends.

"Oh, say, can you see by the dawn's early light, through the bombs bursting in air, and the rockets' red glare, *if our flag is still there?"*

To that tensely anxious question, the story of Prudence Crandall gives a steadfast "yes."

Dorothy Canfield Fisher
Arlington, Vermont
1955

PRUDENCE CRANDALL

January 1833
Canterbury, Connecticut

Marcia pushed back the long curtains and pressed her nose to the windowpane, peering out into the night. Snow was piled against picket fences and house sills; the road was rutted where the stages had passed. Through the darkness the lights in Andrew Judson's house gleamed warmly.

The curtains had not been drawn in the room where company had gathered and Marcia could watch them—the women in their silks, the men in their high white collars. She saw Miss Prudence, her head bent forward as if she were listening intently. Mrs. Fenner was laughing and Mrs. Frost turned to face her husband who was speaking to the group.

Then a clock struck eight and Marcia drew back from the window and went to the fire to blow some life into it. Miss Prudence would be returning soon. She had said she would leave the Judsons' at eight o'clock, no matter how engaging the conversation or how entertaining the company. Marcia hastened to the front door and opened it a crack.

The Judsons' door was open and a stream of yellow light flowed out across the snow.

"Permit me, dear Miss Crandall," Mr. Judson was saying, "to see you to your door."

"Thank you, Mr. Judson, but I hesitate to bring you out into the cold."

"I deem it a privilege, Miss Crandall, to accompany you." He held her cloak, putting it around her shoulders while she fastened the clasp at her throat.

Mrs. Judson smiled affably. "I believe Mr. Judson wishes you lived at the far end of Canterbury, Miss Crandall, so he might have the pleasure of your company for a longer time."

"Indeed, yes," Andrew Judson exclaimed. "Yet I would not have your school, Miss Crandall, be any place but on the Green, across from our stately Meeting House and in the environment of noble homes."

Good nights echoed on the frosty air and the door of the Judsons' house was closed. As the tall, thick-set man accompanied the slender woman along the rutted road, over the piles of snow and onto a neatly swept walk, Marcia opened the door wide enough for a chink of light to fall on their way.

"You have not regretted giving up your work in Plainfield and coming to Canterbury?" Mr. Judson was saying.

"No, indeed! This past year has been richly rewarding."

"Quite aside from what you give in the higher branches of learning to our daughters and to those scholars who come from a distance, Miss Crandall, you must know that we consider you an ornament to our town."

"Indeed?"

"You have created a favorable impression and secured an excellent reputation in the brief span of time you have been here. I speak not only for myself but for all on the Board of Visitors when I say that the school answers our highest expectations."

"Thank you, Mr. Judson. I have no ambition to make learned parrots of my pupils but to qualify them for usefulness in the society to which they were born."

"If there is anything you need, Miss Crandall, any new apparatus for the school, any letters of recommendation to people of influence whose daughters might be in attendance, I am at all times yours to command."

"You fill me with gratification, Mr. Judson. Will you not step inside for a moment? There is a small matter which I would like to bring to your attention, if I do not presume on your time."

"My time is at your disposal, Miss Crandall."

Marcia opened the door and smiled at Prudence Crandall, bowing her head slightly in acknowledgment of Andrew Judson.

"Marcia will take your cloak, Mr. Judson," Prudence said. "Now, let us proceed to the parlor where a fire is burning. May I warm you against your return journey with a cup of hot tea?"

She handed her cloak to Marcia and the girl left the room.

"You have a well-trained servant, Miss Crandall," Mr. Judson said. "It must be a comfort in these days of dissatisfaction with the working classes."

"Marcia is not a servant, Mr. Judson. She is my household assistant. She had been with me for seven years, since she was a child of ten."

"Was she born in this country?"

"Yes, of free parents."

"I see. And does she profess the Christian religion?"

"She is a Christian, Mr. Judson. As a member of our family she has attended Friends Meeting with us in Providence and in Plainfield. Now that I reside in Canterbury, she accompanies me to church every Sunday. I am surprised that you have not seen her with me."

"I fear that my eyes do not always take in the lower orders," Andrew Judson smiled.

Prudence Crandall did not smile. "Sir, I was brought up on plainness of speech and my profession makes it imperative." She sat down, smoothing her skirts with an impatient gesture. "May I ask why you are so interested in Marcia?"

"As President of the local organization of the Colonization Society, I am interested in all free Negroes."

"I know very little about that Society."

"It is worthy of your interest, Miss Crandall. Many men of affairs in both the Northern and Southern states feel that the only answer to the growing power of the Negro is to remove those who are free to Texas or Mexico or some other large territory. I am of those who favor removal to Africa. Negroes who have experienced the blessings of Christianity would then be able to Christianize their fellow Africans."

Prudence looked at Andrew Judson, her lean face intent on his florid one, her blue-gray eyes piercing in their gaze. "Did I understand you to say 'free Negroes,' Mr. Judson?"

"You did."

"Then—" she paused, "would that not continue the institution of slavery?"

"It would." Mr. Judson lifted his hand and pointed it in playful accusation. "Miss Crandall, I believe you must be guilty of reading *The Liberator.*"

"I could not be, sir, for I have scarcely seen a copy."

"So much the better for you. It is a violent sheet,

published in Boston by a young abolitionist of the name of Garrison."

"I must read it."

"I advise you not to, Miss Crandall. Such things are out of woman's sphere."

Prudence opened her mouth to speak, then shut it tight.

"Come, come," Mr. Judson smiled engagingly, "we have had far too pleasant an evening to close it on this distressing subject. You spoke of a small matter, was it—" he paused, "of business?"

"Yes, it was." Prudence went to her desk. Taking an envelope from a drawer, she opened it to remove a letter it contained which she left on the desk. Assuring herself of the remaining contents of the envelope, she returned to Mr. Judson and placed it in his hands. "The money you advanced to me for the school I can now repay. Will you be so kind as to count it before signing the receipt?"

Andrew Judson took the envelope and counted the bills carefully. "You are like a mariner, Miss Crandall, sailing the ship of your school on the sea of prosperity."

"Thank you, sir." Prudence smiled faintly. "I wish whatever I undertake to meet with success and I sincerely hope, Mr. Judson, that you will never have occasion to regret the faith you and your fellow townsmen have placed in me."

"Indeed, we will not, so long as you remember to keep the higher education of womanhood your goal and not venture upon affairs that belong to man's sphere."

Prudence crossed the room and rang the little silver bell that was on her desk. "I wonder, Mr. Judson, how long we will be able to maintain two spheres when the least student of geography knows the world to be one."

"I scarcely see that that has anything to do with the matter."

"Perhaps not, and yet I often find teaching most effective when done with symbols."

Marcia entered the room with a tea tray.

"Another cup, Marcia, please, and ask Miss Almira to join us."

"Miss Prudence," Marcia spoke softly, as if unwilling to have Mr. Judson hear her words, "Miss Almira begged to be excused. She went to bed early with a chill. I have taken good care of her and there is no need for you to feel alarmed."

Prudence turned to Mr. Judson. "May I ask you to excuse me, sir, for a moment? I must see if my sister is comfortable. Please to take your tea while it is hot." She left the room.

Marcia poured a cup of tea and offered it to Mr. Judson. "Is there anything else you would like to have, Mr. Judson?"

"No." He sipped his tea in silence while Marcia put another log on the fire and swept the hearth. As she was leaving the room he called to her.

"Sir?" She turned to face him.

"Tell me, my girl, have you ever thought that you would like to go back to your homeland?"

Marcia stood still in the doorway. "I was born in Connecticut, Mr. Judson."

"But surely your people are in Africa."

"My people?" She stared at him, puzzled by what he was saying. Then she smiled in understanding. "Oh, sir, my parents are dead now. I have no people of my own except Miss Prudence and Miss Almira and their brothers, Reuben and Hezikiah. They live with their father in the south part of the town, and Mr. Crandall has always told me that his home was mine, too."

"But they are white."

Marcia looked at Mr. Judson. Her eyes opened wide. A startled expression came over her face. She twisted her hands together and fixed her eyes on them.

"I might be able to arrange passage on an early ship for you," Mr. Judson went on. "In Africa you could marry someone of your own kind."

Marcia stopped twisting her hands together and let them fall to her sides. She raised her head and looked at Mr. Judson, facing him with level eyes. "Thank you, but I am already spoken for. When Miss Prudence no longer needs me, I am marrying Charles Harris." She turned quickly and left the room.

When Prudence returned, Mr. Judson was standing

in the center of the room, his cloak on, ready to leave.

"Pray, will you not be seated, Mr. Judson?"

"No, Miss Crandall, I must go. Permit me to say one thing. For your own good and the good of the school, I should dismiss that black girl instantly."

Prudence stood her tallest. "Sir, the school is my property now. I shall consult myself on what is best for all concerned."

"Good night, Miss Crandall."

"Good night, Mr. Judson."

Prudence went to her desk and lifted her silver bell, shaking it vigorously. When Marcia reached the room in answer to the summons, she thought it was to remove the tea tray and went toward it.

"Marcia, have you one of those papers that Charles brings you sometimes?"

"Yes, Miss Prudence. He brought the new one last night. I offered it to you this morning but you said you weren't interested."

"Never mind what I said this morning. I want to see it now."

"I'll fetch it right quick."

"One moment, Marcia. Is Sarah Harris spending the evening with you?"

"She was here earlier, Miss Prudence, but I've sent her home now."

"Did she ask to see me?"

"Yes, Miss Prudence, and I told her if she wanted to see you about being a scholar she'd best not bother you any more because you'd already given her your answer and it was no."

"I must ask you in future not to think for me, Marcia. Fetch me the paper, please."

"Will that be all?"

"Yes, that will be all."

Prudence sat down. The letter which she had removed from the envelope was lying on the desk facing her. She picked it up and read it, her fingers tapping slowly as she enumerated the seventeen signatures that followed Andrew Judson's. They were all names of leading men in the life of Canterbury, men whom she had come to respect.

October 3, 1831

To Miss Prudence Crandall—

The subscribers, having understood that you have taken into consideration the propriety of establishing in the village of Canterbury, a school for the instruction of female youth, take this method to signify our entire approbation of the proposed undertaking, and our strong desire in its accomplishment. Permit us to offer you our efficient aid, and our cordial support.

Andrew T. Judson, Esq.

She folded the letter and put it away in a drawer, then she sat quietly, her hands resting on the desk, her eyes looking into the world of her thoughts.

Marcia crossed the room and placed a copy of *The Liberator* on the desk. Prudence picked it up, becoming so engrossed in it that she was unaware of Marcia's presence as she added another log to the fire and laid a shawl across her shoulders. Marcia stole softly from the room. She knew better than to disturb Miss Prudence when she was busy.

Early in the morning when Marcia went to the parlor to ready it for the day, a cry of surprise escaped her. The fire had long been dead. The room was cold, full of the smell from the whale-oil lamp that had burned all night and was still flickering, its flame feeble now against the daylight. Prudence sat at her desk, the shawl hanging loosely about her shoulders, her head in her hands.

"Miss Prudence, haven't you been to bed at all, at all?"

Prudence turned slowly to face the girl. The shawl fell from her shoulders to the floor. She looked at Marcia as if she did not recognize her, as if she had been away on a journey and, coming back to familiar faces, found them strange.

Marcia started across the room, then she stopped. She felt almost afraid to approach Miss Prudence for there was a singular look on her face. She was like one who had been greatly companioned and around whom a glory lingered.

"Aren't you tired, Miss Prudence?" Marcia began.

"Aren't you hungry?" she pleaded, trying to bridge the distance between them with some need she could answer.

Prudence shook her head.

Marcia came nearer and picked up the shawl that had fallen to the floor, folding it neatly over her arm. "What you been doing all night, Miss Prudence?" There were no schoolbooks on the desk, no composition papers or sheets of sums, only the small Bible from which Prudence read to her scholars.

"I've been wrestling with my conscience, Marcia."

"*All* night?"

Prudence nodded. She opened the Bible and read from it to Marcia, "'So I returned, and considered all the oppressions that are under the sun: and behold the tears of such as were oppressed, and they had no comforter; and on the side of their oppressors there was power; but they had no comforter.'" She closed the book. "If those words meant anything when Solomon wrote them, they mean the same thing now; and they mean one thing—not one to me and one to Mr. Judson. I'm beginning to see, Marcia, what I must do."

"Whatever it is, Miss Prudence, I can see that you need something to eat."

"In its time, Marcia. I must go now and talk with Almira. After you have prepared breakfast and warmed the schoolroom, I want you to take a message to Sarah Harris for me."

"Yes, Miss Prudence."

"Tell her that I will see her tonight at seven o'clock. Here, in my parlor."

"Yes, Miss Prudence." Marcia repeated the message, hardly able to believe what her lips were saying and her ears were hearing.

"Here is your paper, Marcia. I found it intensely interesting. You may return this copy now to Charles, but make sure that I see the next one."

Only Marcia knew of the sleepless night and of the message that was to be conveyed, for the day passed as all others in the Canterbury Female Boarding School. The daughters of the town's leading citizens arrived shortly before nine o'clock, hooded, mittened and cloaked against the January cold. Laughing and chatting together, they hung their outer garments in the passage and went in to the classroom to join the girls already there who boarded at the school. When Prudence Crandall entered the room they rose and chorused good morning, and they remained standing while she read to them from the Scriptures. Then they divided into different groups, some to work with Almira, now quite recovered from her chill, some to work with Prudence.

The morning passed in recitation and study. The afternoon was devoted to needlework and, as the girls sewed, the two Miss Crandalls took turns in reading aloud. At five o'clock, the day girls put on their wraps and returned to their homes, while the boarders went to their rooms to rest and prepare themselves for the evening meal. It was a day like all the others; it had an established pattern. There was no reason to believe that the day that followed would be any different.

Shortly before seven o'clock, Prudence settled herself in her parlor to await her visitor; but Sarah Harris did not keep her waiting. As the clock was striking the hour, Marcia and Sarah came down the passage together and stood in the doorway. Sarah was taller than Marcia and her skin was lighter. She carried herself with a reposeful dignity, but there was eagerness in her face and a seeking look in her eyes which contrasted with the other girl's placid manner.

"Here is Sarah Harris, Miss Prudence," Marcia said, remaining in the doorway as Sarah stepped forward into the room.

"Thank you, Marcia. Good evening, Sarah." Prudence held out her hand in greeting. "I will not need you any more this evening, Marcia. You may go now."

Marcia seemed unwilling to leave. "I'd like to make sure you'd get some sleep in your bed tonight."

Prudence laughed. "I shall sleep tonight, Marcia, and in my bed. Never fear." As Marcia left the room, Prudence explained to Sarah Harris, "Last night there was a war going on within my soul and I could find no rest, but today I stand on the side of victory and rest will come easily in its time."

"You must be tired, Miss Crandall." Sympathy was in Sarah's voice and manner.

"On the contrary, I have never felt more exhilarated. Please to sit down, no—not so far away, here, where you will get some good from the fire."

"Thank you, Miss Crandall."

"Do you still wish to become a scholar in my school, Sarah?"

"Yes, I do, Miss Crandall." Sarah looked surprised. "I've asked you so many times and you've always said no, I'd almost given up asking you."

"Why do you want to gain a higher education, Sarah? Did you not learn enough in the District School to satisfy you?"

"I learned to read and write and figure, and that's much to be thankful for; but I want to learn more so I can teach my own people some day."

"Your desire is certainly a worthy one."

"Oh, Miss Crandall, could I learn—" Sarah's eyes had filled with tears of joy and she found it difficult to speak, "could I . . . "

"You could learn anything a qualified teacher presented to you, Sarah, but I have not thought that I could teach you."

Sarah reached out her hands imploringly. "But, Miss Crandall, they say you can teach anybody anything."

Prudence's pale face flushed. "That is not what I

mean, Sarah. Of course, I *could* teach you, but I have not felt that I should."

Sarah dropped her gaze. She did not want to press Miss Crandall for a reason she could guess all too well.

"Something happened to me last night in this room," Prudence went on, "something that made me ask myself searching questions. Why should I not teach Sarah Harris? Why should I not admit her to my school? It took me all night to find the answer."

"Yes?" The girl leaned forward eagerly.

"The search revealed to me that within my own breast I entertained a certain prejudice against the color of a person's skin. I knew that was wrong, but I could not help it. It was there. Knowing how I felt, I knew how anyone else whose daughter came to my school might feel if I admitted a Negro as a scholar." She paused.

"What happened, Miss Crandall? What happened to change you?"

"I read a copy of that paper for which your brother is an agent."

"The Liberator?"

"Yes. In it the condition of the people of color, both slave and free, is so movingly portrayed, the double dealing of the Colonization Society is so ably expressed, and the question of Emancipation so boldly advocated, that I found my feelings undergoing a distinct change."

"Oh—" Sarah drew her breath in sharply.

"I then spent some time reading my Bible and, in the inner light of conscience, overcame my prejudice. I saw then that I would have to act in accordance with my conviction of duty."

"What have you decided to do?"

"I have decided to admit you as a scholar. You may enter my school tomorrow morning. There will be a desk and chair awaiting you."

A smile parted Sarah's lips while tears filled her eyes. She tried to speak, but the words would not come.

"The terms will be the same for you as for the other girls."

"My father is able and willing to pay. Time after time he has told me so."

"That is good. You will be as one of the girls, no special favors, no unusual duties."

Sarah rose to her feet and sighed deeply. "My prayers are answered."

"Or just beginning," Prudence smiled wryly. "The way may not always be easy."

"Book learning comes easy to me, Miss Crandall."

"If that were all!" Prudence exclaimed. "However, several of my scholars are girls you have known before."

"Yes, indeed, Miss Crandall. Many of us knew each other in District School."

"And there was never any unpleasantness, was there? Or any difficulty?"

Sarah shook her head.

"Let us hope there will be none here. Perhaps the battle I fought within my bosom last night will suffice for the township."

Sarah stood up. "Thank you, Miss Crandall. I'll repay you in the work I'll do someday for my own people."

"That is gratification for a teacher," she took Sarah's hands in hers, "to know that the teaching goes on."

Sarah left the room quietly. A few minutes later light steps could be heard running down the stairs, turning into the room.

"Prudence, what has thee done to make Sarah Harris so happy? I saw her in the passage and the smile on her face was like the summer sun."

"I have granted the request she has been making of me for so many months. I have admitted her as a scholar to my school."

"And does thee think this will not cause trouble?"

"What trouble, Almira, could it cause?"

The younger sister shook her head. "I think thee should have spoken first with some of the parents of the girls, some of the patrons of the school."

"I thought of that, Almira, but I decided not to speak to anyone. If I did, it might cause the same opposition to arise in other hearts that arose in mine—the opposition to color."

"But what—"

Prudence shook her head. "Nothing anyone might think or say could alter a decision that it was my duty to make."

"But—"

"If Sarah is admitted to the school and welcomed by the girls who already know and like her, their parents will agree."

"And if they don't?"

"Then we must face the consequences."

Almira smiled a thin ghost of a smile. "Thee belies the name thee was given, Sister."

"And how, pray?"

"By being so headstrong."

Prudence reached out and caught hold of her sister's hands. "When thee is older, thee will find that as conscience dictates, action must follow."

Almira looked at Prudence. Ten years were between them. Ten years of devotion and admiration on the part of the younger, ten years of protection and guidance on the part of the elder.

"I will stand by thee, Prudence."

Fateful Days

The cheerful sound of voices filled the room as the girls clustered by the fire, holding out their hands to catch some of its warmth. It was a cold day, but the sun was bright and, glancing from the snow that lay deep outside, it filled the plain room with light. There was a hush in the voices as steps could be heard in the passage. The girls turned to face the door, expecting to see their teachers.

"Oh, Marcia, so it's you!" a girl exclaimed.

But Marcia was not alone; Sarah Harris stood beside her, smiling shyly at the girls.

"Good morning, young ladies." Sarah turned her head slowly from one to another as the smile widened on her face.

"Good morning, Sarah," some of the girls replied, while others stared at her.

Marcia was a familiar figure in the school; her cap and apron proclaimed her duties and everyone knew how skilled her hands were in household care, how swift her feet in running errands. Sarah Harris, standing there in her long butternut brown dress with its neat collar of tow, puzzled the girls.

"Sarah, have you come to work for Miss Prudence?"

Sarah shook her head and stepped forward into the room, while Marcia nodded to the girls as if her mission had been accomplished and withdrew. "No," Sarah said, "I've come to attend school."

The crowd of girls by the fire were silenced by the news. Some of them who had known Sarah at District School smiled at her politely; others, to whom she was a stranger, lifted their heads and looked away.

"Has Miss Crandall admitted you, Sarah, or did you—" The question trailed into awkward wordlessness.

"Miss Crandall has admitted me as a scholar," Sarah explained, apology in the tone of her soft voice. Conscious of what her presence had done to the roomful of girls, she did not want to intrude more than was necessary.

"Well," the girl sighed, "I suppose we really will have to study now! You always knew more than any of us at District School."

"Oh, no," Sarah shook her head.

"Yes, you did, Sarah," another girl spoke up. "But you were always ready to help us."

"Sarah, I still can't tell the difference between an analogy and an allegory, and Miss Prudence wants us to use both in our compositions next week."

Groans rose from several of the girls as they thought of the work before them.

The youngest of the girls who had been standing by her older sister ran impulsively toward Sarah and took hold of her hands.

"Oh, Sarah," she exclaimed, "your hands are so cold! Come and warm them or you won't be able to open a book." She drew Sarah toward the fire and the cluster of girls parted. "Did you walk all the way from your father's farm?"

"Two miles isn't far and my heart was so happy that my feet felt as if they had wings on them."

"Let's ask father if we can send the sleigh for Sarah on school mornings." The little girl looked up at her sister, but her eager words met with no response.

Some of the girls stepped aside to make more room for Sarah. Others, partly in curiosity, partly in civility, drew near her; but a change had come over them all and it was reflected in the sound of their voices. They had laid aside their earlier bantering mood for one of cool formality. Sarah Harris had won the respect of all those who had known her at District School. The quietness of her spirit with the eager reach of her mind that had impressed them then still had its effect;

but while it was one thing to be with her at the Canterbury District School, it was quite another to have her with them at Miss Crandall's Female Boarding School.

The little girl looked at Sarah. "Perhaps Miss Crandall will make you a teacher here some day!"

The look of tentative delight that had come over Sarah's face when the girls made a place for her by the fire left her.

"Don't say that, please; don't ever say anything like that. It's enough that Miss Prudence has allowed me to be a scholar."

"But you want to teach, don't you?" one of the older girls asked.

"My own people."

"Whatever do you mean?"

There was a pause, then a girl on the edge of the group said in a small tight voice, "She means it's people of color she wants to teach."

For a long moment no one knew what to say. But their spirits were too high and life too exciting for the moment to last, and soon they were talking again, telling Sarah what had been happening to them since they had last seen her and asking her about herself.

"Girls!" Prudence stood in the doorway with Almira beside her. She raised her voice slightly, "Girls!"

The group by the fire became silent, then they turned toward the door. Sarah Harris, who had been sitting on the hearth, rose and smoothed the folds of her dress. She was taller than the others. There was a dignity about her that made her seem older. It was not her color alone that made her different, but the simplicity of her appearance; no ribbon nested in her dark hair, and her dress that fell in straight lines was devoid of tucks or furbelows.

Prudence Crandall bowed to the girls as she stepped forward into the room, followed by her sister. "I see that I do not need to introduce our new scholar."

The girls shook their heads.

"I am glad. Now, go to your seats, please. It is close to nine o'clock. Sarah, your desk is the third one from the left in the second row."

Sarah went to her desk and stood beside it.

"Before we commence our lessons," Prudence announced, "I am going to read to you from the Rules for the School. It is, as you all know, our custom to read these at the admission of a new scholar. Those of you who have heard the words often enough for them to be rooted in your hearts my say them inwardly."

Almira took a book from a wall shelf and placed it on the table, opening it for her sister.

"You are all acquainted with the value put upon silence and obedience, decent behavior and cleanliness," Prudence reminded the girls and her tone was so direct and persuasive that each one who listened wondered if she could ever forget a word, "and in all matters of address remember that the plain language of the Scriptures is to be used. In your hours of leisure, observe modesty and sobriety and use such exercise of body as may preserve your minds in sweetness to each other, that friendship and harmony may dwell among you and you may learn to prefer and love each others' company."

Prudence looked into the faces of the girls, returning their earnest gaze, then she picked up the open book and read from it. The words were so familiar from oft hearing and oft reading that she might have said them, but there were times when she preferred to read from a book. She wanted the girls to know that the authority with which she spoke was not hers alone but had behind it the endurance of the printed word.

"'Never tell a lie or use artful evasion, nor wrong any person by word or deed. Swear not at all, nor use the name of God irreverently or in vain. Mock not the aged, the lame, deformed or insane, or any other person; throw no sticks, stones, dirt, snowballs or any other thing at any person; nor wantonly or unnecessarily at any creature; revile no person, nor utter any indecent expression; never return any injury or affront, but forgive agreeable to the declaration given us by our Lord, Matthew six, verses fourteen and fifteen.

"'In all things, to all people, behave in a modest and civil manner. With your school fellows be humble and obliging, never provoking one another, contending or complaining about frivolous matters. Courteously use the word please or some soft expression when you ask anything, one of the other. Observe to make some grateful return for any little kindness received; never returning injuries but learning to forgive, showing by exemplary deportment how all ought to behave.'"

The voice moved quietly on and the girls' attention was compelled, not through the words alone but because of the esteem felt for the person who spoke the words.

"The objects of education are twofold: mental development and knowledge of facts with their relation to usefulness in life. To the end that the faculties of your minds may be expanded, invigorated, and brought to maturity, my sister and I devote the patient, persevering and protracted effort of our days." Prudence closed the book and sat down.

A girl in the back row put up her hand.

"You may speak."

Rising and standing by her desk she spoke earnestly, "I want to say that we all wish to be worthy scholars."

"The wish can father the work." Prudence accepted the girl's statement. "Now, to the day. Almira, will thee take the arithmetic class in the next room? Those who are reading moral philosophy, and that includes you, Sarah Harris, will remain with me."

The day moved on, following its orderly established pattern. Different groups worked at their studies, gave their recitations, submitted their papers. Reading and writing, grammar and arithmetic, history and geography, all received due attention. At noon the girls went to the dining room where Marcia had a hearty meal waiting for them. When they had finished and until half past one, they were allowed to engage in whatever quiet pursuits they fancied, providing whatever was done would disturb no one; then they returned to the schoolroom.

The day that had been so bright had changed and the wind swinging in from the east with the taste of snow on it, furrowed the sky with clouds. It was Friday, the day the girls went for a walk two-by-two down the village street, with Miss Prudence at the head of the line and Miss Almira at the rear. As the time approached for the outing, Almira endeavored to persuade her sister to forego it.

"We have faced the elements before, Sister," Prudence replied. "Surely it will do the girls no harm to walk abroad even though the wind is raw."

"Will thee excuse me, Sister, and perhaps Sarah could remain in the house with me."

Prudence, swift in her solicitude, reached out her hand to Almira. "Thee had a chill not long ago, has it returned?"

Almira smiled and shook her head. "Thee is thoughtful of me, Sister. Pray think equally of others."

Prudence opened her mouth to speak, but at that

moment two girls entered the room and she never uttered the words that had risen to her lips.

"May we put our cloaks and bonnets on now, Miss Prudence?"

"No, girls. The weather is rapidly becoming inclement. There will be no walk this afternoon."

The hours passed pleasantly: some of the girls sewed, others painted on narrow lengths of velvet that would be made into belts, the two Miss Crandalls took turns reading aloud. At a quarter before four o'clock, Marcia brought tea to the schoolroom. After it had been enjoyed, the final hour of the day was spent in study and preparation for the next week's lessons. Soon after five, Prudence looked up from the writing she had been doing at her table.

"You may return your books and papers to their proper places," she said. After the girls had complied, she went on, "Before you are dismissed, I ask that you retire your attention from the work of the day and that you partake of a few moments of inward recollection. I will call your names for dismissal. Please to leave quietly, remembering that while you may be released some other may be deep in thought."

"Sarah Harris," it was the first name to be called.

The tall, dark girl stood beside her desk. She bowed in recognition of her dismissal and tucking two books under her arm left the room. A few minutes later the door could be heard opening and closing as she went out into the cold of the gathering storm. A rush of wind blew through the schoolroom. Prudence called the names of two girls who rose and left the room.

Singly or in groups they went from the room, the day girls to their homes, the boarders to their rooms. One scholar remained sitting quietly, waiting for her name to be called. Prudence nodded at her.

The girl stood up and smiled. "Miss Prudence, I thought you were never going to call my name, but I didn't mind."

"That is good. You had enough to think about."

"Oh, yes," the girl said, "and it seems as if there's more to think about since Sarah came. Good-by, Miss Prudence, until Monday morning."

She left the house, but in a short time she was back again, struggling to shut the door against the wind that came in with her. She ran across the room and stood beside her teacher, eyes shining and cheeks that had been pale from the long day indoors whipped into color by the cold.

"Miss Prudence, shall I tell my parents that there is a new scholar?"

"Why would you not?"

"They—" the girl hesitated, "they might not like it."

Prudence looked away from the girl's eyes and spoke slowly. "School teaching is of no value if it promote not honesty and candor."

"Yes, Miss Prudence, but—" the voice faltered.

"It is as right for Sarah Harris to learn as for you.

Your parents will not object to anything that is right."

"No, Miss Prudence." She paused, still unpersuaded. "Must I always obey my parents, Miss Prudence?"

"Those who have rightful authority over us we must obey."

The girl turned and walked slowly out of the room.

The storm which had been gathering descended with full force sometime between night and morning. Saturday was a day of whistling winds and tossing snow, but the Crandall house was warm and the two sisters did not regret being homebound. There was always sewing to do. There were the day books to correct which the girls wrote in during the week and turned in on Friday. There were letters to write. By Sunday morning the sky had cleared and paths were being made in the deep snow so people could get to church.

The sisters, with Marcia at their side, made their way across the road and over the Green to the Meeting House, and an hour later they made their way back again. The attendance was sparse and people had huddled in their pews as if to keep what warmth they had to themselves.

Almira's teeth were chattering. "I have n-never known the M-Meeting House to be s-so c-cold," she said when their own door closed behind them.

"We might not have been there for the looks received or the words exchanged," Prudence commented sharply.

"Thee has always s-said one should approach and l-leave the Lord's House in a s-seemly m-manner," Almira reminded. "That is what thee t-tells the g-girls."

"Sometimes the manner can be too seemly."

"Oh, Sister!" Almira flung her arms around Prudence, clung tightly to her for a moment, then she let go her hold and ran from the room.

That evening there was a knock on the door and Marcia opened it to Andrew Judson. He would not give her his cloak but asked to be shown immediately to Miss Crandall.

"Good evening, Mr. Judson." Prudence rose from her chair by the fire and went across the room to welcome him. His eyes were as cold as the air that came in with him and his face was set. The smile on her face faded. She drew her lips together. "Pray be seated."

"Miss Crandall, I will not detain you long and what I have to say can be said standing. My daughter returned from school last Friday evening with some curious information. In the hope that she is wrongly informed, I have come to you. It is not your intention, of course, to admit a Negro as a scholar."

Marcia, standing in the doorway, saw Miss Prudence stiffen, bracing herself as if to face a blast of wind.

"If you refer to Sarah Harris, it is my intention, Mr. Judson, and I have already admitted her."

Andrew Judson let out an exclamation of disgust. "A girl of color among our daughters!"

Prudence remained silent, but her eyes did not

waver from Mr. Judson's face. When she spoke her voice was low and steady. "God gave her her color, Mr. Judson."

"That has nothing to do with the matter in hand."

"It has everything to do with it. What God gives, He gives in trust. I respect black as I do white."

"Miss Crandall!"

"Yes, Mr. Judson?"

"This is certainly a singular departure from your duty. You came to Canterbury to teach our daughters the refinements, and now—and now—"

"Mr. Judson, I see only one duty as a teacher and that is to instill in my scholars the desire of doing to others what they would have done to themselves. I encourage my girls to be diligent and attentive in their studies. The proficiency they attain will be their chief ornamentation."

"You have no right to place this girl on a footing of social equality with our daughters. Such an action is highly insulting."

"Have you forgotten, Mr. Judson, that I was brought up in the Friendly principle of universal brotherhood? To me, slavery has always been a sin; equally sinful is the continued degradation of a race."

"Miss Crandall, with all due regard to the people of color, it has been determined by authorities far wiser than you that they are incapable of rising from their menial condition. This being the case, they should not expect to elevate themselves in Connecticut."

"What would you have them do?"

"Do! Let them return to Africa from whence they came and Christianize the natives remaining there."

"The Christianity shown them here is hardly worthy of export."

"I had not thought to hear such sentiments form your lips, Miss Crandall."

"There is no reason, Mr. Judson, to set Sarah Harris apart from your daughter or any of my scholars. Her deportment is excellent as are her mental powers, and her desire for knowledge is an incentive to all in the school."

"But her color, Miss Crandall."

Prudence was silent, drawing her lips tightly together. She took a step toward Mr. Judson and looked at him intently. "Mr. Judson, if it is a question of her color or my conscience, the choice has already been made."

Andrew Judson turned to leave the room. At the door he paused. "Miss Crandall, you have given great offense. I say only this: you must dismiss Sarah Harris within the week or see the ruination of your school." He would not wait for Marcia to close the door but slammed it behind him.

Marcia stood before Prudence. "I never should have brought Sarah to see you, but she's a good girl. She'll know what you mean when you ask her not to come to school any more. I'll go now and tell her."

"No, Marcia."

"Charles will be there and he may have a new

copy of *The Liberator* for me to fetch back to you."

"Marcia, I have no intention of dismissing Sarah Harris. She will keep her place with the other girls tomorrow—and tomorrow—and tomorrow."

Marcia's lips were trembling too much for her to voice the response of her understanding.

Prudence sighed.

"There is no need, Marcia, to tell Miss Almira of Mr. Judson's visitation."

Marcia lifted her head and swallowed hard. "Miss Prudence, don't you think that Miss Almira knows what people are beginning to say? She doesn't want any harm to come to you."

Prudence laughed. "Why, Marcia, what harm can come to anyone for doing right? You look tired, child. Run along to bed. I'll put out the lamps and see to the fire."

Marcia obeyed, but it was a weary time before she went to sleep. Kneeling in the darkness of her room beside her bed she prayed, trying to hold back tears. "Keep her safe, Heavenly Father, keep her safe. None of us can do anything with her when her mind is set, but perhaps You can."

School opened the next morning and proceeded according to its pattern all through the day. The girls seemed natural, though a little more formal, and Sarah was in all ways admirable. When evening came and the last scholar had either gone home or retired to her room, Prudence sat alone in the schoolroom at her table. Marcia came in to sweep the floor.

"You see, Marcia, everything is quite all right. I knew that the girls could be trusted."

Soon after seven there was a knock on the door and Marcia opened it to Captain Richard Fenner. Prudence, hearing his voice in the passage, wondered if he had come to tell her of some new provisions he had acquired in his store, but the expression on his face when he entered the parlor informed her before his words of the nature of his call.

"Miss Crandall," he said abruptly, "if what I hear is true I must warn you to change your intention."

"For what good reason, Captain Fenner?"

"Reason? Can't you see the harm that may follow if you insist on teaching that girl higher branches of learning?"

"What harm resulted when the apostle Philip taught the treasurer of Queen Candace, even riding with him in his chariot on the road to Jerusalem? The stranger was an Ethiopian."

"Canterbury is not Judea."

"An excellent observation, Captain Fenner."

"I didn't come here to talk ancient history, Miss Crandall. What I want to know is what are you going to do now?"

"Quite possibly I should dispose of my house and remove myself elsewhere."

"Come, come, Miss Crandall," Richard Fenner's tone changed, "that is the last thing we would want you to do. We wish our daughters to continue to benefit by your excellent teaching."

"I see. And I have no doubt that the purchases I make in your store for a household of some thirty people are of some interest to you."

"Indeed, Miss Crandall, I would not like to lose your trade."

"Indeed, Captain Fenner, I would not like to lose my school."

"Then we are agreed?"

"In principle, perhaps, but each one must follow his own course of action."

Before Richard Fenner left, Prudence told him that she expected to go to Boston soon to visit some of the infant schools and to purchase some apparatus for her own school.

"If you would be so kind," she said, "as to give me a letter of introduction to certain of your friends there, I would greatly appreciate it."

"Gladly, Miss Crandall. You shall have the letters tomorrow. Can this mean you contemplate enlarging your school?"

"Yes, Captain Fenner, such is my hope."

Richard Fenner left the house in better spirits than he had entered it, feeling he had accomplished something, yet not sure what it was.

The next night Mrs. Judson and Mrs. Adams came to call, their skirts rustling as they settled themselves in their chairs.

"There's no question but that Sarah Harris is a very respectable girl," Mrs. Judson began pleasantly. "As a servant, anyone would prize her highly."

Mrs. Adams leaned forward in her chair, "But she is hardly the one to be a friend to our daughters, to come into our homes on an equal footing."

"Why?" Prudence's tone was sharp.

"My dear Miss Crandall, can you ask that?"

"I can."

"Well, if you must have an answer, because of her color."

"There is a clear course left to me and that is to go elsewhere," Prudence replied, "though I shall be sorry to do so. I have long entertained the feeling that teaching is best done where it is most needed."

"You have another course, dear Miss Crandall, and that is to dismiss that Negro girl."

"The school may sink, but I will not dismiss Sarah Harris." Prudence's voice held within it the grim firmness of belief that she had been gaining.

On the last night of the week Andrew Judson came again. He managed to smile in greeting and he even sat down in the chair opposite Prudence.

"May I remind you, dear Miss Crandall, of your desire to succeed, voiced to me in this very room not many days ago?"

"I have no desire to succeed at the price of my conscience."

"To fail at your age, if you will pardon my mentioning so delicate a matter, could ruin your life."

"I realize that, Mr. Judson. I have not lived thirty years to no purpose, but I shall not fail."

"You seem very sure."

"The events of this past week have given me assurance."

"Miss Crandall, if you insist on putting your design into execution, you will bring disgrace upon us all."

"Then let us all be strong enough to bear it."

"You will be made the object of ridicule and censure."

"I do not fear such."

"Have you no feelings whatever, Miss Crandall?"

"I have indeed, but my nerves have never been more sensitive than my conscience."

Mr. Judson rose. "It is not our wish to force your decision at this time. I will call on you again soon. If you persist in your desire to keep this colored girl in your school we must withdraw our daughters. Do you understand?"

"I understand."

Mr. Judson laughed harshly as he went toward the door. "Twenty-four white scholars or one black. The decision is yours."

"Mine!" Prudence exclaimed.

The door closed behind him. Marcia entered the room and stood waiting quietly. Almira hastened to join her sister. Prudence flung out her hands to them both.

"Mine!" she repeated, "and he has made it for me." She threw back her head and laughed nervously. Then her laughter faded. The color drained from her cheeks and she reached out to Almira to steady herself. "Oh, Sister, what if they *do* withdraw their daughters? We would indeed face ruin, for the school must be full to pay."

"Take time to think, Sister."

"I have been thinking, all week long. I have—" Her voice wavered into silence, but her eyes were shining as if they saw what words could not yet shape.

Almira touched her hand. "Sister, do one thing for me. While thee is thinking, do nothing to cause offense. Tell Sarah not to return until this matter has been settled."

Prudence did not speak at once, but when she did it was in agreement with her sister's request. "Thee is right, Almira. Nothing will be lost and the school will proceed in its usual way. I must find someone to help thee for I may be obliged to go to Boston."

"Thee said only a week ago that thee was going to visit the infant schools sometime and make a few purchases."

Prudence smiled. "Sometime has become soon."

Marcia shook her head sadly. "Miss Prudence, when will you and Miss Almira take your supper? It's been waiting for you this past hour."

"Give me one half hour, Marcia, I have a letter to write. I think there will be no more callers to disturb us this evening, or again on this particular matter."

Marcia left the room and Prudence sat down at her desk. Almira stood by the fire, holding a book in her hands. "Do nothing in haste, Sister," she murmured, as the sound of Prudence's pen could be heard moving across the paper.

"This is not haste. This is what has been growing in me all week. The more they have said to me, the more certain I have become."

The pen moved on over the paper, the only sound in the room. At last Prudence rose from her chair and went over to stand beside her sister. "Read it, Almira."

Almira took the letter and read—

Canterbury, January 18th, 1833

Mr. Garrison: I am to you, sir, I presume, an entire stranger, and you are indeed so to me save through the medium of the public print. I am by no means fond of egotism, but the circumstances under which I labor forbid my asking a friend to write for me; therefore I will tell you who I am, and for what purpose I write. I am, sir, through the blessing of divine Providence, permitted to be Principal of the Canterbury (Conn.) Female Boarding School. I received a considerable part of my education at the Friends' Boarding School, Providence, R.I. In 1831 I purchased a large dwelling house in the centre of this village, and opened the school above mentioned. Since I commenced I have met with all the encouragement I ever anticipated, and now have a flourishing school.

Now I will tell you why I write you, and the object is this: I wish to know your opinion respecting changing white scholars for colored ones. I have been for some months past determined, if possible, during the remaining part of my life, to benefit the people of color. I do not dare tell any one of my neighbors anything about the contemplated change in my school, and I beg of you, sir, that you will not expose it to any one; for if it was known, I have no reason to expect but it would ruin my present school.

Will you be so kind as to write by the next mail and give me your opinion on the subject; and if you consider it possible to obtain 20 or 25 young ladies of color to enter this school for the term of one year at the rate of $25 per quarter, including board, washing, and tuition, I will come to Boston in a few days and make some arrangements about it. I do not suppose that number can be obtained in Boston alone; but from all the large cities in the several States I thought perhaps they might be gathered.

I must once more beg you not to expose this matter until we see how the case will be determined.

Yours, with the greatest respect,
Prudence Crandall

Almira handed the letter back to her sister. "And thee will go to Boston to see Mr. Garrison?"

"Yes, I shall go as soon as I receive a favorable reply."

"It will be cold in Boston, Sister."

"But not so cold as in Canterbury."

Marcia's voice could be heard calling them to supper. The two schoolteachers picked up their skirts and ran like schoolgirls down the passage.

A Round of Visits

A young man made his way along Washington Street as quickly as slush and snowbanks and thronging people would permit. From time to time he looked up at the house numbers. When he reached a lighted doorway that bore over it the words, THE MARLBORO HOTEL, NO. 229, he turned and went up the steps. It was warm inside and the lights seemed bright after the twilit darkness of the street. He peered before him as if he did not see well, then went toward a stove at one side of the room. Coals were gleaming behind the isinglass doors and he held his hands toward the warmth. In a moment or two he unwound the muffler from his throat, unbuttoned his coat and reached into a pocket for his glasses. Hooking the steel bows behind his ears, he gazed around the room. There was no one present except a clerk writing at a desk. Behind him was a clock indicating the hour was approaching six. The young man took a letter from his pocket and read it. It was dated Boston, January 29.

> *Mr. Garrison: The lady that wrote you a short time since would inform you that she is now in town, and should be very thankful if you would call at The Marlboro Hotel and see her a few moments this evening at 6 o'clock.*
>
> *Yours, with the greatest respect,*
> *Prudence Crandall*

Returning the letter to his pocket, he went toward the desk. "You have a Miss Crandall of Canterbury, Connecticut staying with you this evening?"

"Yes, Sir," the clerk replied, his eyes still on his work. Looking up he stared at the man before him. There was something familiar about the high brow with its thinning hair, the prominent nose, the sensitive mouth. It was a face he had seen before. He smiled with recognition. "Yes, indeed, Mr. Garrison."

"You know me then?"

The clerk pushed aside the ledger in which he had been writing. "I am familiar with your words, Mr. Garrison," he said, placing his hand on a copy of *The Liberator* that lay on the desk, "and your likeness is known to all those who feel for their fellow men. I am honored to meet you. You are expecting to see Miss Crandall?"

"Yes, at six o'clock."

"If she does not appear soon, I will send a message to her room. She and her companion arrived early this afternoon and they seemed in need of some rest. The roads are rough and rutted this time of year and passengers on the stages are generally quite shaken by the time they arrive."

At the sound of footsteps, Mr. Garrison turned. A woman was entering the room. She was tall and slender, dressed simply in gray. Her fair hair was cut short and brushed neatly away from her forehead. Her nose was too long and her chin too prominent for her to be beautiful, but there was a quality about her that removed the awareness of physical aspect. Something serene and indomitable had come into the room, and as no one had entered but the woman in gray, it must have come in with her. Following her, and now stepping forward to stand beside her, was a young girl who seemed all of a color; her dress was as brown as her skin and her curly hair was only a shade darker.

William Lloyd Garrison needed no introduction. Quickly he stepped forward, holding out his hand. "Miss Crandall, I feel certain."

Prudence walked toward him and took his hand in a firm clasp. The swift passage of a smile across her lips caused them to curve for a moment, but almost instantly they returned to the firm line of one who had long ago disciplined herself. "Mr. Garrison," she said, "it is indeed an honor to meet you. Your writing has struck answering chords within me. This is my companion."

Mr. Garrison took Marcia's hand in his, a soft warm hand in comparison to Miss Crandall's.

"Your time is valuable, Mr. Garrison, and I will not presume to take much of it," Prudence went on with the air of one who wasted no time in preliminaries. "Shall we sit over there on the sofa? The questions I have to ask can soon be answered."

"My time is at your disposal, Miss Crandall. The worthy purpose you have in mind stirs me deeply. Did you have a pleasant journey?"

"It was rough and cold and the coach was crowded. However, since the purpose of a journey is to get one to a destination it was successful. Pray, be seated, and let us come to the point."

"The matter you refer to in your letter, Miss Crandall, makes me feel that you have in your mind the welfare of our colored friends."

"Not in my mind only, Mr. Garrison, but in my heart. All my life I have had a hatred of slavery, instilled by my parents and by my upbringing. I have long wanted to do something to aid the cause of abolition. Wealth is not mine to give, but what I have is the ability to teach."

"Nothing could be of greater benefit to the Cause," Mr. Garrison nodded approvingly.

"I have been teaching with considerable success for the past ten years, in Plainfield and now in Canterbury. In future I would like to devote myself to colored scholars."

William Lloyd Garrison leaned toward her, his young eager face working quickly. "What gave you this idea, Miss Crandall?"

"A time comes to us all when we must put our theories to the test and let action attest belief, Mr. Garrison. For months past, a most respectable young colored girl in Canterbury has begged me to admit her to my school. I have now admitted her."

"With what result?"

"The town is disturbed and the parents of my white scholars threaten to withdraw their daughters."

"I can hardly say that I am surprised," Mr. Garrison smiled grimly. "Now you are considering closing your school to one color and opening it to another?"

"Yes, if I can obtain sufficient scholars. I have, Mr. Garrison, invested all my property in the school. My father, who is a farmer, invested a good deal of his substance in preparing me for my life's work. I cannot afford to fail."

Mr. Garrison was silent, but the movement of his fingers indicated that he was counting. "There are several families in Providence who would prize a higher education for their daughters," he said. "I know of one or two in New York and New Haven and at least one in Philadelphia." He smiled encouragingly. "There might even be some in Boston upon whom you could call while you are here."

"I will do so tomorrow if you will give me letters of introduction."

"Miss Crandall, if the admission of one colored scholar to your school has caused trouble, the trouble may multiply as you add more scholars."

"I think not, Mr. Garrison, if I close the school completely to white girls and open it to the daughters of our colored friends."

"I hope you are right, but I warn you to be prepared. Feeling is running high between the champions of Anti-Slavery and the advocates for Colonization. The battle has only just begun and the Colonization Society will take every occasion to make an issue of an event. Your school may be in the front line of attack."

"I fear you flatter my school unduly, Mr. Garrison. It is very small, and Canterbury is only a country town."

"When do you propose to open your school to colored scholars?"

"With the new term, on the first of April."

Mr. Garrison took a paper from his pocket and started to write on it. "I will do all I can to help you, and so will *The Liberator*."

"I wish no publicity, Mr. Garrison. Can you promise me that?"

"I cannot, Miss Crandall. The school that seems small to you may prove to be the spark that will ignite a flame of feeling. The story of your brave venture may be told from rostrums and pulpits; it may be retold in the journals of our land. Because you are a woman and an educator, not a politician or a man of business, people will notice and heed."

"Mr. Garrison, please—"

"Only remember, Miss Crandall, that two million Negroes are still in subjection." He pushed back his glasses that had slipped down his nose. "This question of education is vital. Too long our colored friends have been held to manual knowledge and denied the more excellent branches. They must all rise as they are able, as any of us must do likewise, to intellectual and moral worth. If denied the right to education, what other rights may not be denied them?"

He leaned toward her earnestly, the passion of his feeling bringing color to his cheeks and a burning intensity to his eyes.

Prudence lowered her gaze to her hands that lay folded in her lap.

"Miss Crandall, the cause of free men everywhere demands that you accept the challenge!"

"Mr. Garrison, I have always felt that education was the instrument for improvement. Now, I am convinced." She looked at him, her blue eyes clear and steady. "With such as I have, I give myself to the Cause."

"We must move quickly then. I have been jotting down names of people who would be interested to know of the new arrangements you plan for your school. It will mean a round of visits for you."

"I am prepared to make them. The school is well cared for in my absence by my sister."

"How long shall you remain in Boston?"

"Only as long as it is necessary. I plan to visit some schools and make certain purchases for my own."

"I trust you are not too tired to attend Arnold Buffum's address this evening. He is expected to make a great appeal to the female portion of the audience."

"I am never too tired to do anything that is in the line of duty, but pray tell me of this gentleman."

Mr. Garrison laughed. "I know him so well that I think others do, too! He is the principal lecturer for the Anti-Slavery Society, a man of great gifts and an even greater heart."

"I will be there."

"Then I shall be able to introduce you to many who will support you. I trust that Samuel May will also be there."

"Mr. May! His pulpit is in Brooklyn, Connecticut, which is near to Canterbury. I have heard him spoken of as a fearless preacher."

"He is a staunch supporter of the Cause and will

stand by you if you meet with any difficulty."

"Mr. Garrison, I do not expect any difficulty, and I trust I can gird myself against fear."

"Ah, Miss Crandall, you must do what I do! When my friends are full of apprehension for me I tell them that I cannot know fear, that it is impossible for danger to awe me."

"Fear, then, is a luxury in which I shall not indulge." Prudence rose from her chair. The interview was at an end.

They walked together across the room to the door of the hotel. "Tell me, Mr. Garrison," Prudence asked, "do you think that I have a chance to succeed in this undertaking?"

"Success means much to you?"

"Yes, it does," she answered honestly.

William Lloyd Garrison tied his muffler slowly around his throat, then he took off his glasses and put them in his pocket. When he turned to her it was with the vague glance of the far-sighted who see no near object well. "Sometimes devotion to a cause demands the sacrifice of everything that means most to us." He placed his hand on the doorknob and turned it. "Good night, Miss Crandall." The door closed behind him.

Prudence joined Marcia who was standing by the stove, gazing dreamily into the little leaping flames behind the isinglass doors.

"What did you think of him, Marcia?"

Marcia roused herself from her revery. "I feel as if I could listen to his voice for a long time."

"Yes," Prudence agreed, "it is compelling."

"He's like a captain of a ship, Miss Prudence. It seems he's always looking ahead to the land his ship's a-sailing to. Oh, Miss Prudence, he's not going to make you do anything against your will, is he?"

"No, Marcia," Prudence shook her head, "I could not feel more strongly or see more clearly. I shall do what seems right to me. No coin in any land could make me barter that privilege."

Marcia nodded. She knew what Miss Prudence meant.

"Now, Marcia, please to fetch my cloak and bonnet. We must leave soon if we are to be in time for Mr. Buffum's lecture."

"Seems as if we just got to Boston," Marcia said, "seems as if my bones were still aching, seems as if—"

Prudence made no reply. Taking from the pocket of her dress a little notebook, she began jotting down in it an outline of work for the school that would open on Canterbury Green, on April first.

Some two weeks later Prudence Crandall and Marcia returned to Canterbury, tired from their travels, but heartened by the reception they had had in the homes of colored people and among the many friends of Mr. Garrison, in Boston and Providence. All had enthusiastically given their support. Prudence began to see that her plans for a school were part of the tide that was moving across the nation, gaining pace and force. "No one can move events faster than the tide," she had commented to Marcia, "but there are always those who must ride the first waves."

A few days after her return she sat at her desk and wrote a letter.

Canterbury, February 12th, 1833

Mr. Garrison: I can inform you that I had a very pleasant passage home. Arrived here Saturday evening about 8 o'clock; saw Mr. Packer on Monday; told him the object of my visit to Boston. He said he thought the object to be praiseworthy, but he was very much troubled about the result. He is fearful that I cannot be supplied with scholars at the close of one year, and therefore he thinks I shall injure myself in the undertaking.

If you have not yet sent on to New York the information you intend, I would thank you if you would do it immediately, for I am expecting to take the next boat for New York and shall be in the city early on Friday morning. I have not the least acquaintance there, but a friend of mine will give me an introductory letter to Mr. Miller, one of the colored ministers in the city.

The evening after I left Boston I called on Mrs. Hammond in Providence. She soon collected some of her friends, among whom were Mr. George

Benson and a brother of his, who appeared to possess hearts warmed with fellow-feeling and awake to the cause of humanity. They engaged to do all for me in their power, and I have no doubt they will. Saturday morning called on Mrs.. Hammond again, and she walked with me to the residences of three families of color, with whom I was much pleased. They seemed to feel much for the education of their children, and I think I shall be able to obtain six scholars from Providence. When I return from New York, I think I shall be able to lay the subject before the public.

Yours, etc.,
Prudence Crandall

Undaunted by winter roads and sea winds, Prudence, with Marcia to accompany her, left for visits to New York and Philadelphia. There she called on people to whom Mr. Garrison had given her letters, and others whom she had heard would be sympathetic. Everywhere she was received cordially and in one home after another she found the same deep desire for learning. Appreciation for what she was doing went often beyond words. Full eyes and warm handclasps spoke for grateful hearts. The promise that on the appointed first day of April, the daughter in whom were such hopes, would arrive in Canterbury, meant as much to Prudence Crandall as any evidence on paper. Willingness to pay the tuition was such that Prudence might have returned to her home with the money due her for the first quarter, but she had no desire to take even a token payment before her scholars were under her roof.

Some of the girls were daughters of men of wealth; all were supported by parents or relatives able to pay their expenses. Only one of the girls came from a family with no means to pay the tuition, but when Prudence visited the girl in New York she found her so worthy and promising, that she accepted her. A neighbor, eager to see the girl succeed, offered to pay all the expenses involved.

"I was a slave," she told Prudence, "and purchased my own freedom not many years ago. I know what education will mean for this young girl."

Another girl, one of the oldest interviewed by Miss Crandall, was then keeping a small school in New York, but she was aware of her need for more learning. By spare living and hard work she had saved enough money which would permit her to attend the Canterbury school for half a year; a friend came to her aid with additional funds, so she might round out the year.

The two travelers returned home satisfied with the journey: Marcia to resume her housework, Prudence her teaching.

The strokes of Prudence's pen were swift and sure as she wrote out for insertion in *The Liberator* the announcement that would inform the reading public of the change in her school.

Happy at the prospect, she was proud of the success she had had, of the importance of the men who were her patrons, of the way in which she had reached out to include scholars from most of the principal cities on the eastern coast. But it was with a laggard pen that she wrote out her remarks to her scholars for the last day of school. So guarded had she been about her travels, saying only that they were in the interests of the school, and so carefully had Almira worked with her, that no one had suspected a change was in the making.

On Friday afternoon, March first, the day before *The Liberator* would appear with her notice in it, she addressed her girls for what she knew would be the last time. "It is not only the end of the day and the end of the term," she told them, "it is the end of the school in its present form."

Twenty-four faces were upturned to hers. Twenty-four pairs of eyes gazed at her trustingly, expectantly.

"Today the school is closed. An end is ever a new beginning, and on April first the school will re-open to young ladies and little misses of color."

The eyes still gazed at her. Lips parted, but no words broke the silence in the schoolroom.

"I hope we may remain friends, though we shall no longer be teacher and pupils. Each one of you will always be dear to me—" she paused, turning her face away from the intentness of the eyes that were fixed on her. Swallowing against emotion, she went on. "You are dismissed. The day girls will take their belongings and go to their homes. The boarders will retire to their rooms and start packing their trunks. Arrangements have been made for the stages to stop tomorrow morning."

No one moved. No one spoke.

"Please to leave as you are, in a body, not separately as is customary." The sound of Prudence Crandall's voice was tight and strained.

There was a shuffling of feet, but still no one moved.

"The test of teaching is in the practice made of what has been taught," she said, her voice becoming more natural as she became their teacher again. "Obedience is no more one of the lessons of this school than it is of life," she reminded them.

A girl in the front row drew in her breath sharply. She left her seat and ran toward Prudence standing by her table, stern of face, erect of bearing. The girl reached up with her arms and flung them about her teacher. She clung to her for a moment, then with a sob that could be heard through the room she tore herself away. Blinded by tears, she stumbled out to the passage where her bonnet and cloak were hanging, then she ran out the front door not waiting to close it after her. The other girls followed her example, forgetting decorum in their love for their teacher.

With quick nervous gestures Prudence smoothed the disarray of her collar and swept her hands over her short hair. "I think I could endure better the jolting of the Providence stage than the loosened emotions of the girls."

"Thee must not let bitterness get a hold, Sister," Almira said gently, as she came toward Prudence from her place by the door.

"I love them all, Almira, but I may not see any one of them again." Prudence turned away from her sister's eyes, trying to fight back the feelings she did not want to show. "Oh, Almira, why should I feel like this when it is my duty I am doing?"

Almira lifted Prudence's hand and held it against her cheek for a moment. "The surgeon's task is always hard, dear sister."

"Miss Prudence! Miss Almira!" Marcia stood in the doorway. "Charles has just come from Providence with an early copy of *The Liberator*. He says there's something in it you'll want to see. He says Mr. Garrison sends his respects."

Marcia crossed the room and placed the paper on the table.

Prudence started almost as if she had not seen it before. There it was, crying defiance at the evils of slavery, challenging public opinion with flaming words. OUR COUNTRY IS THE WORLD—OUR COUNTRYMEN ARE MANKIND said its masthead, and Prudence knew that now and forever after she was identified with those words. She felt as if she had stepped away from the peaceful countryside in which she lived, into a world where the wind blew harsh and cold. But it was a quickening wind, and the life it fostered was one in which good things were to be shared by all, not a privileged few.

The sisters bent over the paper, turning a page, scanning long columns of fine print.

"There it is, Sister!" Almira said. "Read it, read it aloud, and would that all the world could hear!"

Prudence took the paper into her hands.

She read in a clear and resolute voice the words she herself had written—

PRUDENCE CRANDALL,

Principal of the Canterbury, (Conn.) Female Boarding School,

RETURNS her most sincere thanks to those who have patronized her School, and would give information that on the first Monday of April next her School will be opened for the reception of young Ladies and little Misses of color. The branches taught are as follows:—Reading, Writing, Arithmetic, English Grammar, Geography, History, Natural and Moral Philosophy, Chemistry, Astronomy, Drawing and Painting, Music on the Piano, together with the French language.

☞The terms, including *board, washing*, and tuition, are $25 per quarter, one half paid in advance.

☞Books and Stationary will be furnished on the most reasonable terms.

For information respecting the School, reference may be made to the following gentlemen, viz:—Arthur Tappan, Esq., Rev. Peter Williams, Rev. Theodore Raymond, Rev. Theodore Wright, Rev. Samuel C. Cornish, Rev. George Bourne, Rev. Mr. Hayborn, *New-York City*:— Mr. James Forten, Mr. Joseph Cassey, *Philadelphia, Pa.*:— Rev. S. J. May, *Brooklyn, Ct.*:—Rev. Mr. Beman, *Middletown, Ct.*:—Rev. S.S. Jocelyn, *New-Haven, Ct.*;—Wm. Lloyd Garrison, Arnold Buffum, *Boston, Mass.*:—George Benson, *Providence, R.I.*

Canterbury, (Ct.) Feb. 25, 1833.

When she came to the end, Almira said quietly, "So thee takes up the challenge."

"I had not thought, when conscience spoke to me a few short weeks ago, that it would make me choose such a difficult way."

"Conscience does that, but it gives courage, too."

Prudence lifted her head. "So, this is courage then? Doing what one knows one must without thought of consequences."

The next night the house was empty of girls, for the boarders had gone. The stage that whirled over the turnpike between Norwich and Worcester had taken some, and the stage that ran between Hartford and Providence had rumbled off with the rest. Prudence and Almira sat in the parlor reading when a knock sounded at the door. Marcia went to answer it.

"Mr. Adams and Mr. Frost," she announced in a voice loud enough for the sisters to hear who their callers were. She peered out to see if there were more to come. "Captain Fenner and Dr. Harris." Beyond them was the night, windy and raw.

The four men went into the parlor. After greetings had been exchanged they lost no time in coming to the purpose of their visit.

"The news that has broken upon the town fills us all with alarm, Miss Crandall," Mr. Frost, as spokesman, began. "A public meeting of citizens convened only a few hours ago and we have come to convey our sentiments to you."

"It will interest me to hear them," Prudence replied.

"We protest the establishment in our midst of such a school as you intend."

"I am indeed sorry to hear that, gentlemen, but I fear that my plans cannot now be changed. I am under engagement to receive twenty pupils on April first. My arrangements have all been made."

"Miss Crandall, have you thought of what may happen to the town should these girls become public charges?"

"That is not likely, gentlemen, for the girls come

from families of moderate if not substantial means."

"But if they should?" Mr. Adams persisted.

"To quiet the fears of those who are apprehensive that my scholars ever might become chargeable, the patrons of the school hold themselves in readiness to give bonds in any amount that may be required, to secure the town from such harm."

"Can you not see, Miss Crandall," Dr. Harris began guffly, "how far flung the reaction to this may be? How can we afford to educate those who can never profit by it?"

"If you believe in education at all, Dr. Harris, you cannot deny it to Africans. Have they not the same right we all have to enlarge their sphere of usefulness?"

"Certainly, Miss Crandall, but their sphere is manual work. I have great regard for the people of color, but I know that our district schools supply all the education necessary or advisable."

"And you feel they should have no further opportunity?"

"I do," the doctor said emphatically. Then his face reddened, "I mean, I do not."

Prudence drew her lips together. "Your intent is clear, Dr. Harris, whatever your words."

"Miss Crandall," Mr. Frost leaned toward her, "have you considered the dangers that may follow upon these leveling principles should you be successful in introducing them into Canterbury?"

"Dangers?" She repeated the word as if it were

new in her vocabulary and she would try the sound of it.

"Yes, Miss Crandall, the dangers of educating people beyond their station."

"I must ask you to be more precise, Mr. Frost."

Mr. Frost glanced at the other members of his committee, but their faces were set. He dropped his voice. "There is always the possibility—" he paused.

She shook her head. "I understand plain language, Mr. Frost. I have no gift for circumlocution."

He dropped his voice still lower. "Surely you do agree that there is a difference between . . ."

Captain Fenner cleared his throat. "As a member of the committee in charge of the Meeting House, Miss Crandall, I am obliged to ask that you do not bring your colored girls there on Sunday mornings. Such intrusion would be offensive."

"I will do nothing to disoblige the town, Captain Fenner, and I shall not willingly offend."

Mr. Frost stood up and the others followed his lead. "Good night, Miss Crandall. It is clear that since reason cannot prevail over you, we must resort to other means. A town meeting will be called at the earliest possible moment to devise and adopt such measures as will avert this nuisance you contemplate, or speedily abate it if you persist in bringing it into our environs."

"Gentlemen, I will agree to any fair proposal to remove my school, but my right to teach colored pupils if I see fit I will not relinquish. Good night."

With no further words the Committee of Protest turned and left the room. The sound of the door closing after them put a period to their visitation.

Town Meeting, March 9th

Marcia left the group seated by the table, who were still lingering over their breakfast, and went to the window. The roads were filled with the traffic of people coming to Town Meeting. There were men on horseback, men in carts drawn by oxen, men in gigs drawn by horses; they came not from Canterbury alone but from outlying farms and neighboring towns. The Green before the Meeting House was no longer white with snow; churned by wheels and trampled by hooves, it was deep with mud.

The day was warm and sunny. Marcia opened the door to let some of the fresh spring-like air into the house. A man, trudging along beside his oxen, saw her standing in the doorway and stopped. Marcia watched him as he leaned down, groping for something on the ground. When he straightened up, she shut the door just in time to keep the well-aimed snowball, packed with mud, from coming into the house. She felt its thud as she put her shoulder against the door. What the man said as he flung it she did not hear, for the group around the breakfast table were rising, and the sound of the voices, mingled with the scraping of chairs, filled her ears.

"You must know, dear Mr. May, what your letter meant to me."

"Miss Crandall, the least I could do was to assure you of my sympathy and support," Samuel May was smiling genially.

"Would that I might attend the Meeting, but since it is not seemly, I am fortunate indeed to have you and Arnold Buffum to act in my behalf." Prudence looked resolved and tranquil. The effect of years of discipline was evident in her words and on her countenance.

"I feel sure," Arnold Buffum said, "that when we have put your case before the Meeting they will understand your motives."

"If they will listen," Almira spoke quietly.

"The laws of our land permit each person's voice to be heard," Samuel May remarked.

"Explain to them how I was led to take the step which has given such offense," Prudence urged. "How I could not consent to their demands to dismiss

Sarah Harris without wounding her feelings, and that I would not do lest it add to the load of injuries our colored friends bear."

"It is our hope, Miss Crandall, that the falsehoods circulating about your intentions will be brought to an end by this Meeting."

"Your hope and my prayer! I beg of you, dear friends, to persuade my townsmen that the sole object of this school is to instruct the ignorant and to fit and prepare teachers for the people of color, that they may be elevated and their intellectual and moral wants supplied."

"That we will do with all our abilities," Samuel May assured her warmly.

"Mr. Garrison says you must be sustained at all hazards," George Benson spoke eagerly, "for if the school is put down here, other places may partake of the panic and prevent such institutions. First and last, he said, all true friends of the Cause must meet this proscriptive spirit and conquer it. Everyone in Boston is greatly excited at what is taking place in Canterbury."

"Mr. Garrison and I have similar sentiments," Prudence replied. "Now, if you will excuse me, gentlemen, I have letters for you to present to Mr. Asael Bacon, the Moderator, begging his permission to let you speak for me." She left the room.

Almira looked at the three men, her gaze resting on one, then another. "Pray have a care for your safety, gentlemen. Since my sister's notice appeared in *The*

Liberator she has been grossly insulted and even threatened with violence."

"Of that I am aware," Samuel May said. "I myself was threatened with personal danger if I so much as appeared in Canterbury today."

George Benson tapped the notebook in his pocket. "Whatever happens will be reported in *The Liberator*, and I shall see that it is well reported!" His eyes flashed and he glanced toward the door, impatient to get to the Meeting.

Arnold Buffum smiled kindly at Almira. "We are not the only ones determined to support your sister. There is law enough in the land to protect her, and I have been told that she has already drawn to herself more praying friends than the population of Canterbury."

Prudence returned with the letters, giving one to Mr. May and one to Mr. Buffum.

"Gentlemen, you know my stand, and you are empowered to enter for me into any agreement you see fit with the citizens of Canterbury. If they will take my house off my hands, pay me what I paid for it and cease from molesting me, I will procure another house in a more retired part of the town. But I will not abandon my project."

"We know your stand."

"It would be difficult to see how they could object to so reasonable a proposition," George Benson remarked.

"Ah, my dear young man," Arnold Buffum turned

to him, "you do not know to what ends the Colonization Society will go! Remember the affair at New Haven two years ago. That was enough to make us bow our heads, not so much in shame as in prayer."

The three men went out the door together and down the walk.

"Marcia," Prudence called sharply, when she saw the mark the snowball had made on her front door.

"I'm coming," Marcia said, hurrying from the kitchen, with a bucket of warm water and a scrubbing brush.

"Please to remove that filth."

"Yes, Miss Prudence, I can do that all right, but I don't know about the rest."

Prudence stepped out on to the walk and looked back at the front of her house. It was pock-marked with mud-packed snowballs. She turned around quickly, looking up and down the road. The town seemed empty of inhabitants. On the Green there were horses tied to trees, and oxen with drooping heads, while like the rumbling of distant thunder came the sound of voices from within the building, as people waited for the Meeting to commence. Prudence went back up the walk, passing Marcia on the steps. "We must wait for the rain to wash the house front. Do what you can with the door."

Almira was standing inside the doorway. She looked at her sister questioningly.

Prudence smiled grimly. "If we have nothing worse than muddy snowballs thrown at us we can endure."

"Sister, look at the conveyances! Hear the hum of voices! Never before have so many people come to Town Meeting!"

"It is a fine day, and so warm. They have enjoyed leaving their farms and firesides."

"It is because of thee."

"No, no," Prudence laughed, "they will find other affairs to talk about before the Meeting is adjourned."

"Thee has become the Canterbury affair."

"A pity, then, that I cannot be present!" Prudence tossed her head and put her hand to lift her skirts as she went up the stairs.

When Prudence had gone, Almira approached Marcia, busy at her scrubbing. "Marcia, give me your brush," she said in a low voice, "and do you cross the road to bring us news of the Meeting. I would know when our friends speak if they are listened to."

Marcia wiped her hands on her apron.

"Take your cloak, child, for you may be there a long time. I will see to your duties."

"Yes, Miss Almira," Marcia said, as she prepared to do what she was told.

Marcia hurried across the road. The windows of the building were set too high for her to peer in through them, but she found a pile of snow in a shadowed corner that had been packed hard throughout the winter and scarcely so much as softened by the sun. She climbed up it and pressed her face against the windowpane. Some children seeing her did likewise, but their curiosity was soon satisfied and they ran back to tasks or play. Marcia stayed on the snow pile, though her feet ached with cold and her fingers grew numb from their hold on the narrow sill.

All she could see at first was a mass of faces, for the floor and the galleries were packed with men sitting and standing. With her nose pressed flat to the glass, she peered around the room searching for familiar faces. She smiled when she spied Mr. Benson and Mr. Buffum with the Reverend Mr. May between them, sitting in a wall pew on the side aisle next to the deacon's seat.

Mr. Bacon, the Moderator, was reading the Warning and when he finished he turned to Rufus Adams. If the room had been silent during the Warning it was even more so for the reading of the Resolutions, and the words came to Marcia, muffled by the pane of glass, but unmistakable in their meaning:

> *Whereas,* it hath been publicly announced that a school is to be opened in this town, on the first Monday of April next, using the language of the advertisement, "for young ladies and little misses of color," or in other words, for the people of color, the obvious tendency of which would be to collect within the town of Canterbury large

numbers of persons, from other States, whose characters and habits might be various and unknown to us, thereby rendering insecure the persons, property, and reputation of our citizens. Under such circumstances our silence might be construed into an approbation of the project.

Thereupon, Resolved, That the locality of a school for the people of color, at any place within the limits of this town, for the admission of persons of foreign jurisdiction, meets with our unqualified disapprobation, and it is to be understood that the inhabitants of Canterbury, protest against it, in the most earnest manner.

Resolved, That a Committee be now appointed, to be composed of the Civil Authority and Select Men, who shall make known to the person contemplating the establishment of said school, the sentiments and objections entertained by this meeting, in reference to said school—pointing out to her the injurious effects, and the incalculable evils, resulting from such an establishment within this town, and persuade her to abandon the project.

Mr. Adams paused and looked out into the sea of faces. He had not long to wait for a sign of feeling. Cheers and an excited stamping of feet rolled fast upon his words.

Marcia wanted to call out in protest, but instead,

she beat her hands on the windowsill and then almost cried with the pain, as her numbed fingers came alive.

Andrew Judson, as Clerk of the Meeting, rose to speak. By far the most prominent man in Canterbury and a leading politician in the state, he commanded instant attention. The people, stirred by his words, murmured and whispered so much among themselves that the sound was blurred and Marcia caught only portions of the speech.

"The idea of having such a school is insupportable—reckless hostility—determined to thwart—property no longer safe—break down natural distinction between black and white—would you have that?"

"No!" the crowd roared. The sound echoed through the building and hammered against the window glass.

"A dire calamity faces Canterbury—Prudence Crandall author of a plot—powerful conspirators engaged with her—school to become auxiliary in the work of immediate abolition—*Liberator* for mouthpiece—open door here and Connecticut will become Liberia of America—appeal to all good men—true Christians—loyal Americans—preservation of liberties—shall we surrender to any other nation or race?"

"No! No! No!" the people shouted, rising in a body to give their words more force. There was a clapping of hands and a stamping of feet. Red of face and breathing heavily, Mr. Judson sat down and took his handkerchief from his pocket, holding it up to his face.

When the people sat down again, one man remained standing.

The Moderator acknowledged him. "You have the floor, Mr. White."

George White looked directly at Andrew Judson. "I propose, sir that a committee be formed to purchase Miss Crandall's property. I, for one, would like to assist in—"

A voice from the gallery shouted "No!"

Mr. White continued speaking, but against the boos and hisses that filled the room, his words were not heard.

The Moderator turned to Mr. Judson for some indication of procedure.

Mr. White raised his voice but the Moderator did not hear or was unwilling to heed amid the confusion of sounds that filled the room.

Samuel May and Arnold Buffum rose from their seats and approached the Moderator, handing him the letters Prudence Crandall had given them. Mr. Bacon glanced at them and turned them over to Mr. Judson. His eye swept the pages, then he crumpled them in his hands and rose to his feet, addressing the people with vehemence and gaining instant attention.

"Fellow citizens, I appeal to you again! These men bear letters from Miss Crandall. They wish to speak in her behalf, but their request is an insult, as they are foreigners. What right have they to interfere in our affairs? Should men from beyond the limits of Canterbury have voice at a Canterbury Town Meeting?"

"No!" a near-thousand voices sounded like one.

"Only tax-paying citizens can take part here!" someone shouted.

Several men rose to their feet, facing Mr. May and Mr. Buffum as they returned to their seats. Angry protests at the violation of custom resounded.

"What right have foreigners here?"

"Who let them in?"

"Throw them out!"

"Order! Order!" Mr. Bacon shouted. Then he turned to Mr. May. "You may speak after the Meeting, but not during it."

"Sir," Samuel May replied in a voice that was courtly and precise, "we do not ask leave to address the Meeting. Miss Crandall asked leave to be heard through us, her sex forbidding her to advocate her own cause."

"Down with the intruders!" a voice roared from the gallery.

"You may speak after the Meeting," Asael Bacon repeated. Then he addressed the room, "Now, are we ready for the vote?"

A man sitting near the front rose and spoke heatedly against the school, then he swung around and faced Samuel May, doubling his fists and shaking them at him. "If you dare to open your lips again we will inflict upon you the utmost penalty of the law!"

"Or something more immediate," his neighbor shouted.

"Order!" Mr. Bacon commanded, and the room that had been seething and restless became quiet. During the silence, Mr. Judson handed a slip of paper to Mr. Bacon who read it in a voice that all could hear, "Moved, That we disapprove the school and pledge ourselves to oppose it at all hazards."

The motion was seconded as soon as it was uttered and when put to the vote a volume of sound rolled from floor to gallery, "Aye!"

If there was a dissenting voice it was drowned in the stamping of feet that followed.

Andrew Judson rose and surveyed the people that packed the floor of the Meeting House. His eyes moved from one side to another, then he raised them to the gallery so no one would be missed. "I declare the vote to be unanimous," he announced.

A motion to adjourn was lost in the roar of sound that echoed from floor to ceiling.

"The Meeting is adjourned," Mr. Bacon said.

The words had scarcely been spoken when Samuel May sprang up and stood on the seat where he had been sitting. "Men of Canterbury! I have a word for you, hear me!" he shouted, and so surprised were the people, that for a brief moment they seemed willing to listen. "You refused to let me present Miss Crandall's story to your Meeting. Justice demands that you hear it now."

Some of the crowd started toward the door muttering angrily, others turned to listen. Marcia, straining her ears to hear, felt tears rise in her eyes as the confusion in the room took away any possibility of her hearing what Mr. May was saying. A sentence came clearly now and then, sometimes a word stood forth, for his voice was powerful and searching as he replied to false statements about the purpose of the school and the character of the proposed pupils. With the dignity and grace that marked him, he related the actual facts and assured the people of Miss Crandall's willingness to dispose of her home on the Green and move to a less conspicuous part of the town.

"Men of Canterbury, I am no foreigner but an American citizen like yourselves, and I ask you to uphold Miss Crandall in her venture. So doing, you will secure to your town high praise for being first in a great labor of love."

Briefly and with energy Mr. May spoke; the moment he stopped Mr. Buffum rose. The brilliant, much-traveled lecturer for the New England Anti-Slavery Society was used to speaking before turbulent crowds. With swift impressive words he told the people of the great issues that were at stake. "Town rights are not so important as the eternal principles of Truth and Justice—what may seem to be local is intimately connected with the greatest question our nation has to decide."

He compelled attention, and though the building

was less than half full when he began to speak, the remaining people were drawn to him. But even his words, reasonable and appealing as they were, could not hold back the tides of hate and fury that encircled the Meeting House.

A group of six men appeared at the door, headed by Dr. Harris. They marched up the aisle to stand before Mr. May, Mr. Buffum and Mr. Benson, while Mr. Judson and Captain Fenner started to close the doors of the building.

"This building is to be cleared at once, by order of the Committee." Mr. Judson announced.

"Out! Out!" people began to shout, milling angrily around the three visitors.

George Benson, who had been writing rapidly in his notebook, closed it and put it safely in his pocket so no harm might come to his account of the Meeting.

"Clear the house!"

"Bolt the doors!"

The six trustees of the Meeting House surrounded Arnold Buffum and demanded that he cease speaking.

"We have the charge of this house," Dr. Harris said, "and we order every one out that the doors may be closed."

Arnold Buffum looked at Samuel May. Samuel May returned his glance with a smile whose meaning was clear.

"We yield to the law," Arnold Buffum said.

Marcia slid down from her snow pile. She stood still for a moment, unaware of cold feet and tingling hands, for the anguish she felt in her heart. Slowly she made her way across the Green and around to the back door of the Crandall house. But she had words to deliver and she could not stay long in the comfort of her kitchen. She went to the parlor where the sisters were sitting, and spoke quickly of what she had seen, wanting to spare her words but knowing instinctively that the more she could acquaint Miss Prudence with the business of the Meeting, the better it would be.

"Thank you, Marcia," Prudence smiled faintly.

"Anyone might think I'd brought you good news, Miss Prudence."

"You have, Marcia, in that you have made me deeply aware of the part I have been called on to play."

"It is no small part, Sister," Almira said, half in pride, half in fear.

"Thee is right, Almira. The contest for impartial liberty that agitates the nation is what is taking place in Canterbury today." She turned her head to listen, as voices could be heard outside, then she said in a low voice, "Sister, perhaps we shall not teach history only, but make it!"

Marcia hastened to the door to open it to George Benson and Arnold Buffum. Almira ran to the window and drew the curtain aside. "Look, Sister! Mr. May and Mr. Judson are crossing the road together.

Perhaps they have come to some agreement."

Prudence crossed the room to stand by the open window with her sister. They were soon joined by the two men. All four stood silently. Samuel May and Andrew Judson had stopped at the Crandall gate and what they were saying came clearly across the space and in the window.

"Mr. May, our acquaintance in the past has ripened almost to friendship. I trust you will remember that the warmth with which I have expressed my feelings has nothing to do with you personally."

"Of course."

"Surely you must realize what a disastrous effect such a school would have in the center of our village! Canterbury would no longer be a desirable place of residence, the value of real estate would go down, there would be a general decline in prosperity."

"Mr. Judson, if you had allowed Mr. Buffum and myself to speak, you would have found that we had not come in a contentious spirit but that we were ready to settle the difficulty with yourself and your neighbors peaceably."

"We are not merely opposed to the establishment of that school in Canterbury, Mr. May, we mean there shall not be such a school anywhere in this State. The colored people never can rise from their menial condition. They are an inferior race and Africa is the place for them. Let them be sent back to their fatherland."

"Mr. Judson—"

"You and your friend, Garrison, have undertaken what you cannot accomplish," Andrew Judson interrupted. "The condition of the colored population can never be essentially improved on this continent. You are fanatical. You are violating the Constitution of our Republic which settled forever the status of the black men in this land. Let them be sent back to Africa or kept as they are here. The sooner you Abolitionists abandon your project, the better it will be for all concerned."

"There never will be fewer colored people in this country than there are now, Mr. Judson, and of the vast majority this is their native land as much as it is ours. It will be unjust, inhuman, to drive them out or make them willing to go by our cruel treatment. Besides, it would not be practicable."

"I cannot agree with you, sir."

"Nor I with you," Samuel May smiled. "The question, Mr. Judson, is whether we will recognize the rights God gave them as men and encourage and assist them to become all He has made them capable of being, or whether we will continue wickedly to deny them the privileges we enjoy, condemn them to degradation, enslave, and imbrute them. I trust, sir, you will come to see that we must accord them their rights or incur justly the loss of our own. Education is one of the primal, fundamental rights of all the children of men. Connecticut is the last place where this should be denied."

"Miss Crandall's school shall not be allowed in Canterbury, nor in any town of this State."

"How can you prevent it?"

"We can expel her pupils from abroad under the provisions of our pauper and vagrant laws."

"And we will guard against them by giving your town ample bonds."

"We will get a law passed by the Legislature forbidding the institution of such a school."

"It will be an unconstitutional law and I will contend against it as such. If you pursue in the course you indicate, Mr. Judson, I will dispute every step you take, from the lowest court in Canterbury up to the highest in the United States."

"You talk big!" Andrew Judson exclaimed with disapproval. "It will cost more than you are aware of to do all that you threaten. Where will you get the means to carry on such a contest at law?"

"Mr. Judson, I myself do not possess the pecuniary ability, nor have I consulted any one yet, but I am sure there are enough lovers of impartial liberty, enough enemies of slavery in our land, to sustain Miss Crandall in her undertaking."

Andrew Judson made an exclamation of disgust.

"From one quarter or another I assure you, Mr. Judson, the funds needed to withstand your attempt by legal means to crush this school, will be found."

"I will have no more of such talk." Andrew Judson

turned away abruptly and without another word crossed the road toward his house.

Samuel May watched him go, then he pushed the gate open and walked up the path. "I wonder if I shall ever meet that man again except as an opponent!" he exclaimed.

When he caught sight of the group standing by the window, he quickened his steps. Prudence and Almira met him at the door. Taking hold of his hands they led him into the room where the others were waiting.

"There is no need for any of you gentlemen to fill the time with talk of recent events," Prudence said, "for Marcia brought us an account of what took place at the Meeting and we have all heard what has just been said at the front gate."

"Would that my words could go round the world!" Samuel May exclaimed.

"But not Mr. Judson's," Almira remarked.

George Benson spoke up, "Even his, Miss Crandall, for to air both sides encourages fair appraisal. *The Liberator* shall have an exact account of this from my pen for their next issue, and if any of the pro-Colonization papers report it, we shall print their comments as well."

"Is there nothing Almira and I can do?" Prudence looked at the men who had done battle for her that morning.

"There is everything you can do," Arnold Buffum

assured her, "and it will best be done by standing firm."

"Mr. Judson may have legal weight on his side, but you have the fiery voice of *The Liberator*'s editor," George Benson said, "and Garrison's columns will ever be ready to march in your defense."

"Please, Mr. Benson," Prudence laid her hand on the young man's arm, "I would not want Mr. Garrison to write of the school more than is necessary. I shun notoriety."

"I know how you feel, dear Miss Crandall," Arnold Buffum's tone was consoling, "but what we shun we cannot always escape."

The faint tinkling of a bell could be heard in the distance.

"Marcia has dinner ready for us," Prudence said. "You must be in need of refreshment, gentlemen."

They went to the dining room and took their places at the table.

Arnold Buffum turned to Prudence and continued as if there had been no interruption. "No longer are you a teacher of a school, you have become part of a great Cause." He reached forward to put his hand on his glass. "In this clear water, may I propose a toast to Prudence Crandall and her sister, Almira—heroic standard bearers in the fight against slavery!"

He put the glass to his lips, but the smile left his face. He held the glass to his nostrils, then said hastily, "Gentlemen, put down your glasses; this water is not fit to drink."

"The town of Canterbury has always had good water," Prudence said apologetically, raising her glass. An odor assailed her and she put it down again. "I beg your forgiveness, gentlemen, I do not know what could have happened."

Marcia could be heard running through the passage, calling their names. She burst into the room. "Miss Prudence—don't drink the water—don't—don't—"

All sitting at the table turned and faced the wide-eyed, frightened girl.

Regaining her breath, Marcia gasped out, "Mary just came in and told me—she heard her people—speaking at table—during Town Meeting—one of them came by with a load of manure—shoveled some into—your well. Oh, Miss Prudence, you might have all been made sick!" Marcia put her apron up to her face and began to cry.

Almira rose from the table and went to Marcia, putting her arms around her. "There, there, be comforted, child, no one has been harmed."

"Almira," Prudence said, "there is a jug of whey in the kitchen."

"Yes, Sister."

"Pardon this interruption, gentlemen. I hope you will not object to drinking something other than water."

"Whey was always my boyhood's favorite," Samuel May said. "What memories its taste will recall!"

There was silence around the table as Almira removed the glasses and put clean ones in their place, which Marcia filled with the cloudy, sharp-smelling whey.

Samuel May looked at Prudence. "I fear, dear lady, that it will be a long time before the water from your well will be fit to drink."

She nodded her head, then said quietly, "So, the siege has begun."

Five days later the Civil Authority of the town—nine men headed by Andrew Judson—called on Prudence Crandall. They lost no time in acquainting her with what she already knew, the vote of the recent Town Meeting. As they presented the Resolutions that had been accepted, they offered their reasons why she should relinquish her plan.

Prudence faced them calmly, refusing to yield.

As a last resort, Mr. Judson suggested that certain responsible men of the town would offer her the sum she had paid for her house if she would completely abandon her project.

"That, gentlemen, is the one thing I will not do. The challenge has been thrown down in Canterbury, the battle must be fought out in Canterbury; though I will gladly remove my school to a less public location."

"You are determined then to proceed?"

"Never more so. My course is set, gentlemen. I can but keep to it and trust the winds of God to fill my sails."

The School Reopens

By the close of the first day in April, twelve scholars had arrived; some were brought by their parents, some traveled alone. With a clattering of hooves and a swirling of dust, the stage from New York had drawn up to the carriage block and stood still while its passengers got out and their trunks, roped to the top, where unloosened and carried in to the house. Skirts fluttering and bonnets streamers waving, the girls had gone to the door to be welcomed by Prudence and Almira, and shown to their rooms by Marcia. An hour later the stage from Providence arrived and discharged its passengers.

The day was warm and sunny, birds were singing and the grass was a bright green. The girls ran through the house, looking from the windows at the leafing trees, gazing across the road at the Meeting House, so stately and serene, telling each other delightedly that was where they would be going on Sunday.

"Seems nice to have the church so near, just a little walk across the road," Ann Eliza Hammond sighed happily as she looked from a window. "It makes it seem as if the Kingdom of Heaven itself were right close at hand."

"Why are there so many carts on the Green, Miss Prudence?"

"And horses tied to the trees?"

"The townspeople are holding a Meeting today," Prudence replied. "Some of them come from farms that lie at a distance."

"When may we go out and play?" Maria Robinson asked.

"Yes, yes, when may we?" several of the girls chorused, jumping up and down with joy at the prospect, after the confinement of traveling.

"Not today. This is a school for young ladies, I would ask you to remember, not a playing place for children."

"Yes, Miss Prudence." They subsided.

The April twilight came down gently over the rounded hills, and the little town of Canterbury drowsed under the early stars. The air was sweet to breathe with the scent of blossoms that rested on it, and there were sounds sweet to hear, as frogs chimed in the marshes and late birds called. Prudence, lighted candle in hand, went through the rooms in which the girls had been tucked into their beds by Almira. They lay still and reposeful under their white sheets with only their dark faces showing, for nightcaps trimmed with lace or ribbon covered their heads. Occasionally the candle caught the glint of a wakeful eye and a quick exchange of smiles was made.

Almira followed her sister like a shadow, then went into the schoolroom with her to see that all was in readiness for the morrow. On each desk was a neatly sharpened quill pen and a small bottle of ink; beside these was a notebook made by Almira, its pages sewed with linen thread and its cover of wallpaper bearing a girl's name.

Presently a heavy dull sound could be heard as of something being rolled across a floor and set in place. The sisters hurried down the stairs to the kitchen where Pardon Crandall stood in the doorway, with his son Reuben beside him.

"Daughters, there is the barrel of water, drawn fresh and clear from the spring and losing none of its coolness as it came the two miles from the farm."

Prudence ran toward her father and kissed him lightly. "Our thanks, and thanks from the girls now under my roof."

"They need not know whence it comes," Pardon went on, "only that they have pure water to drink. It is the living water you will be giving their minds that matters most for them. Ah, daughters," he smiled at them, "were pride not a sin I would be proud of you both!"

"Love is no sin, Father." Almira put her arms around him and kissed his weathered face.

"Look, sisters!" Reuben opened a basket he had over his arm. "The shad came up the river today and I caught these for you. There is one for every one under your roof and two over."

Prudence gazed at the basket of fish. "Now I know that spring has come since the shad are in the river. Thank thee, Reuben."

"Daughter, will thee send a message to me when thee needs more water?"

"Yes, Father, but it will not be for a few days. The shallow well here in the kitchen will serve our necessity; the spring water we shall save for drinking."

"That is good. When we come again we will bring thee a barrel of flour as well as some sugar. There is enough butter from our own cow's milk and eggs from the flock to share with thee."

"Oh, Father, how did thee know we would have need of such things?"

"I heard talk in the town that the merchants would not sell thee any goods; but thee shall not lack, daughter, as long as I have my strength and the land its yield. Come, Reuben, we must be on our way before moonrise. Darkness is a worthy cloak."

"A cloak for kind deeds," Almira said softly, as she and Prudence stood in the kitchen doorway and watched the two men get into the wagon and drive down the road.

An hour later the sisters were in their bed in the room they shared. Almira soon fell asleep but Prudence lay wakeful, planning work to be done the next day and thinking of the days ahead. The frogs in the marshes ceased their chiming. Wind was no longer riffling the leaves of the trees. Silence held the world in its embrace.

Prudence breathed deeply, but with the night air she drew in no balm for her spirit. An uneasy feeling pervaded her as she lay still in the bed, wanting to make no move that might disturb her sister. And then, out of the silence and through the softness of the night, she heard it—the sound which she had known would come. She wondered if she had been waiting for it, steeling herself against it. Hearing it released something within her, though she clenched her hands together under the sheet and stared with wide eyes into the darkness of the room.

It was the sound of creeping feet, of the gate opening and finding its latch again. There was a muffled whispering, then a crackle and spatter against the walls of the house and the windows of the schoolroom. Running feet could be heard and the gate opening and closing again.

When all was quiet, Prudence got out of bed, put

on her shoes and threw her cloak over her shoulders. She went down the stairs, out the front door and around to the side of the house. The windows of the schoolroom had been the target for a volley of eggs. Dripping yolks streamed down the glass; broken shells littered the ground.

Sudden fury gripped her as she surveyed the wantonness and the waste; then she set her lips in a firm line and went back into the house. From the kitchen she fetched a pail of water and a long-handled brush; from the passage a chair to stand on. Working alone, she cleaned the windows and picked up the scattered shells. The girls should not have their first morning marred by such rudeness.

"Yes, darkness is a worthy cloak," she murmured to herself, as she went back into the house. Returning to her bed, as quietly as she had left it, she lay still waiting for sleep to come.

There was peace in the schoolroom that first morning and quiet in the town. Rain fell gently, dropping from the eaves of the house, from the leaves of the trees, graying the near world and veiling the distant hills. Everyone was content to stay indoors, and the girls turned willingly to their books.

Prudence began the day by reading the Rules for the School. When she closed her book and laid it on the table before her, she spoke briefly to the girls about the value and the responsibility of an education. There was not one present who did not feel but that the words were addressed intimately to her.

"To admire the virtues is what we all enjoy," she said, "to practice them is what we all may learn to do. Ann Eliza, please to recite such virtues as you deem worth acquiring and then exhibiting."

The slender seventeen year old girl from Providence stood by her desk and repeated not what she had learned, but what she knew. "Faith, hope, charity."

"Yes. Those are the Christian virtues. Is anyone able to give me the virtues Plato acknowledged?"

There was silence in the room, then a hand went up tentatively.

"Yes, Emila?"

"Fortitude, temperance, justice—and—" the girl hesitated.

"You may say it." Prudence nodded encouragingly.

"And—prudence."

"Right. So we have seven virtues, but these do not embrace all the virtues. We shall discover more as we learn more."

A hand went up. Prudence indicated that the girl might speak.

"Please, Miss Prudence, is it a virtue to be pretty?" The voice had an inquiring tone and its owner could not by any standard lay claim to beauty.

"Women should dignify and adorn society." Prudence replied. "If beauty is theirs, it is a gift from their Maker and is to be cherished as all gifts, but it should not be sought except through the mind."

"Is learning a virtue?" Eliza Weldon asked.

"Only if it leads to wisdom and usefulness. You are here to learn to use your minds, not for the purpose of exhibiting your knowledge, but to help others." She glanced at the intent faces before her. "Yes, Sarah, you have a virtue to contribute?"

"Submissiveness?" Sarah Harris asked quietly.

"Thank you. You have expressed what is for us all of real importance. Now, open your notebooks and take your pens in hand."

As the girls complied, Almira moved from one to another, correcting the hold of a pen, straightening the position of a book, giving to each girl as she passed, a smile or a pat on the shoulder.

"In your best penmanship," Prudence continued, "write on the first page the title of the book—*Depository of Valuable Sentiments*. Place your own name a little lower on the page. Blot the ink carefully and turn to the next page. These books will contain your exercises in composition. In them you will also summarize the books you have read, inscribe passages for meditation, and display your penmanship. When you have completed your first page, dip your pens and return your gaze to me."

There was a scratching of pens and the sound of deeply drawn breaths as the girls bent to their task. One by one they surveyed their work, turned to a fresh page and looked up at their teacher who stood erect and still before them.

"I shall read to you, slowly, so no one need feel hurried, words that I wish you to write on the second page of your Depositories and to refer to every day, until they are written in your hearts."

"Yes, Miss Prudence," the sibilant sound filled the room with their willingness.

"'Young ladies should not murmur at expostulation,'" Prudence read slowly as she had promised. "'They should be accustomed to expect and to endure opposition. It is a lesson with which the world will not fail to furnish them; and they will not practice it the worse for having learnt it the sooner. It is of the last importance to their happiness even in this life, that they should early acquire a submissive temper, and a forbearing spirit.'"

Except for the rain streaming down the windows and the slight scratching sound of the pens, silence ruled in the room. One by one as they came to the last period, the girls laid down their pens.

Elizabeth Henly put up her hand.

"Yes, child?" She was the youngest scholar and small for her years.

"I can understand about submissiveness for us blacks, but isn't there a different word for you whites?"

Prudence did not answer her immediately. She looked away from the small questioner as if in search of the right reply. When she spoke it was with clear and simple directness. "In this school, Elizabeth, there are no distinctions. We shall not use the words black and white except as adjectives."

"Yes, Miss Prudence." The girl sat down satisfied, though her question had not been answered.

"Now I would ask someone to name for me one of the greatest of the virtues, one that endures throughout our lives."

Five hands signaled their eagerness to respond. Prudence indicated Maria Robinson as the one to speak.

The girl stood up. "Obedience." She pronounced the word as if she were sure of its correctness and then sat down.

"You are right. Obedience: to God, to conscience, to those in rightful authority."

After supper when the girls met in the schoolroom for meditation and prayers before they went to bed, Prudence asked Almira to lead them.

"Willingly, Sister. What does thee wish that they should think about on this first night? Duty?" As Prudence did not answer, Almira made another suggestion, "Religion?"

Suddenly Prudence flashed one of her rare and radiant smiles at her sister. "On happiness, Almira. Let us meditate on happiness, this first night."

That first week in April was a rainy one. The girls, longing as they were to go out and discover their new environs for themselves, had to be content to watch them from the windows. Except for the stages that splashed over the roads, a few farm wagons with their loads well covered, and an occasional passerby hugging himself within his cloak, the life of the town was within doors, too. Prudence was glad. Enforced inactivity seemed a small price to pay for peace. As one rainy day followed another, she hoped that the townspeople might become accustomed to the new dwellers in their midst and accept them amicably.

By Saturday the weather cleared and the sisters took their young ladies out for a walk. Neatly bonneted and walking two by two, with their hands clasped before them, the girls received permission to converse only with the one nearest and to unclasp their hands only when it was necessary to lift their skirts from a puddle in the road. Prudence walked at the head, Almira at the rear, and a decorous line they made as they came from the house and moved slowly down the path and through the gate. Scarcely had they turned on to the road when a stone sailed through the air, followed in a moment by a volley of pebbles, nicely aimed to strike the sweeping skirts. Several of the girls cried out in surprise, but as Prudence said nothing and kept walking straight on and Almira only murmured "Eyes forward," the girls followed the example of their teachers.

A troop of boys ran along beside them, barking and whistling, but as no attention was paid them, they soon ran off to find other distractions. From behind the newly leafed bushes jeers came. A window opened and a catcall resounded. Then the window was shut before a face could be seen. It was not until the demure little line had proceeded beyond the houses that the song of birds could be heard, and the breeze. After they had walked what Prudence thought was a proper distance, she turned and they started back.

Almira ran forward. "Sister, may we not cross the fields and approach the house from the rear? The grass would be little wetter than the road."

Prudence shook her head. "We must meet the disturbance, Almira, not run from it. They were only boys who knew no better."

Almira placed her hand on Prudence's arm and looked at her imploringly. "Will not thee stay here with the girls and let me go ahead? I will knock on the doors of the houses and ask the parents to restrain their children."

"Save thyself suffering where thee can, Sister. Thee will not find many to answer a knocking, nor will they put a check on what they wish to see done. We must show them what we are made of. Take heart."

Almira lifted her head bravely as she returned to her place at the end of the line.

When they approached the village and walked by the houses, they were greeted again with hoots and jeers. Someone blew a horn from behind a tree. Another volley of stones was aimed at the billowing skirts.

Prudence quickened her pace as they approached

the gate and some of the girls at the end of the line started to run forward. They were all eager to reach the shelter of the house. Many of them were frightened and some had their dresses badly spattered by the stones.

They had almost reached the house when Prudence suddenly stood still and the girls behind her came to a halt. She turned and faced them. The firmness of her face was familiar to them, but there was a new look now—a fierceness.

"Turn, girls, instantly. Almira, please to lead them in by the kitchen door."

As the girls followed Almira around the house, Prudence stood in front of the steps trying to shield them from what assailed her eyes and nostrils. On the steps and against the front door a load of barnyard refuse had been dumped—manure and feathers, a dead cat, chicken heads and feet. Prudence turned her head away as a wave of nausea swept through her. Then she unclasped her shawl and laid it over the steps to cover the filth as best she could. Breathing deeply and trying to fight off the retching within her, she went to the kitchen door where Marcia met her.

"Miss Prudence, I was here in the kitchen making supper and never saw it until just now from the window. I'll get a shovel and clean it up."

"No, Marcia," Prudence said through tight lips, "it is too much for you to deal with. Reuben will be here tonight and he will remove it."

"Yes, Miss Prudence."

"He can put it around the lilacs," Prudence said, now in possession of herself. "It will help them grow."

"Oh, Miss Prudence," Marcia burst out, stamping her feet with feeling, "I hate the people of this town! They have no right to do these things to you. I—"

"Marcia," Prudence compelled the girl's attention, "this evening I would like you to meet us in the schoolroom for prayers."

"But—my dishes?"

"You can do them later."

"Yes, Miss Prudence."

As Prudence went up the stairs she met Almira coming down. The younger sister's face was strained. Horror had written itself across sweetness and serenity.

"Sister, the girls are in their rooms. They are frightened. Who could have done such a monstrous thing?"

"I do not know, Almira. I think I do not want to know."

"Surely thee cannot go on!"

"Go on? Dear sister, we have scarcely started."

"Then thee will not send the girls to their homes?"

"No, Almira, each one of them is needed here."

"How can they learn their lessons against such things as have happened today?"

"Perhaps, Almira, it will be from such things that they will learn their greatest lesson." Prudence put out her hand to steady herself against the railing.

"Thee is pale, Sister. The events of the day have undone thee, too."

"I shall not be with thee for supper. Read to the girls while they eat, Almira, so they may regain their calm, then conduct them to the schoolroom for prayers."

"And thee—when will thee eat?"

"Later, perhaps. I—I cannot eat now."

"Thee will lead the prayers tonight?"

"Yes." Prudence went on up the stairs. At the top step she called down to her sister. "Almira?"

"Sister?"

"Tonight Mr. Garrison is staying with Samuel May. After Father and Reuben come with the water, let thee and me take the horse and drive to Brooklyn for an hour. All here will be safe with our two men in charge."

Almira's expression of amazement melted into solicitude. "Does thee feel like journeying abroad tonight after what has happened today?"

Prudence threw back her head, her nostrils widened as if she were breathing deeply of an air that seemed to be coming to her alone. "Never have I felt more like it!"

After supper the girls filed silently into the schoolroom and sat down at their desks. They were followed by Almira and Marcia who stood near the door. Prudence was sitting at her table, her head bowed in her hands. When the last shoe had scraped the floor and the last skirt had fluttered into silence, she looked up and into the faces of the girls. Her eyes—steady, fearless, commanding—met theirs that were frightened or tearfilled, dulled with quenched fury or evasive. She spoke to them in a quiet, low voice and her words were at times so soft, that the girls had to strain to catch them.

"We have seen strange deeds done today, deeds that might cause us all to wonder; but we shall forget them in time, both in their unpleasantness and their inconvenience. However, such deeds, by the faculties within us, can be transformed into tools and we can use them as a farmer would his hoe and rake to weed the ground and prepare it for sowing. If the things that happened today caused anger and hatred to rise in our minds, we have need to use them as tools that the growth of forgiveness and benevolence be not choked. I expect you to rejoice with me in deeds such as these, that make us look within and discover what it is that is fruiting in our minds."

Prudence looked at the girls, one by one.

"Now, let us have a time of quiet. I do not wish anyone to leave this room who has not forgiven deeply and entirely the deeds done this day. I do not mind how long you remain here, I mind only how you leave."

Almira was the first to leave, gliding quietly from the room and into the next, where she began to light the lamps. Marcia soon followed her, picking up her skirts and running up the stairs to light candles and ready the girls' beds for the night. One by one they left, smiling shyly at their teacher as they went from the room. Only Ann Eliza Hammond remained.

"Seems as if I never could forgive them for what they've done to you," she said, her voice heavy with bitterness.

"That, Ann Eliza, is always the hardest part of forgiveness."

"But you are *white,* Miss Prudence!"

"Sometimes I wish I were not. Then I know that because I am, I must do what I can."

"Seems as if each one of us has a load to tote. You have yours, Miss Prudence, why should you take all our loads on your shoulders, too?"

Prudence did not reply. Her eyes no longer looked into those of the girl before her but across the room that was shadowy with April twilight.

After another moment, Ann Eliza got up and left the room.

An hour later the Crandall sisters were driving to Brooklyn in the farm wagon behind the plodding mare. The trials of the day disappeared with the distance and by the time they reached the May parsonage they were laughing and chatting in high humor.

Samuel and Lucretia May greeted them warmly. Reverend Levi Kneeland had ridden over from Packerville. Helen and George Benson were there. Mr. Garrison had come from Boston.

"So, you have opened your school and are

resolved to persevere?" William Lloyd Garrison said to Prudence, taking her hand in his and shaking it warmly.

"Yes, Mr. Garrison."

"You are indeed a wonderful woman, as undaunted as if you had the whole world on your side!"

"You must tell us how you are faring," Samuel May said, as his wife brought cups of tea to the visitors.

Prudence and Almira between them told of the first few days of the school and the peace that had reigned within doors. Prudence tended to make light of the disturbance their first walk abroad had caused; but Almira saw to it that nothing was left out. Retiring in her nature, she became bold with pride when she told of how Prudence inspired the girls. "And not with bravery alone, gentlemen, but to forgiveness."

Mr. Garrison listened eagerly as if he were taking notes in his mind of all that was said.

"This must be reported in *The Liberator*!" he exclaimed with conviction. "The world must know what you are doing in Canterbury. The hearts of our sympathizers will glow with fellow feeling and our opponents will surely know discomfort."

"I would prefer, Mr. Garrison, to have the events of the school not be subject to the public eye."

"People must be informed of your work, dear Miss Crandall, both those in favor and those against."

Prudence shook her head in remonstrance.

"Think of all that our colored friends have suffered, Miss Crandall," Mr. Garrison went on. "The end of slavery is drawing near and valor such as yours will hasten the day of freedom."

"Sir, if you must write of the school, may you do so with moderation."

"That," Samuel May commented, "is not an easy virtue for Mr. Garrison to assume."

"Why are you so desirous of moderation, Miss Crandall?"

"The prejudices of the people of Canterbury are greatly stirred and I entreat you to handle them with all the mildness possible. Everything severe will tend to heighten the flame of malignity amongst them. Soft words, Mr. Garrison, turn away wrath, but grievous words stir up anger."

"I make no promises, dear lady, other than to use all my powers and the columns of *The Liberator* in your behalf."

"The results of Canterbury's most recent Town Meeting shall be made known in *The Liberator*," George Benson said. "You have heard of them, Miss Crandall?"

"I knew there was such a Meeting on April first but that was the day our girls were arriving and I gave it little heed. I shall be glad to be informed of any decisions made by the town."

George Benson took his notebook from his pocket.

"They placed it on record, Miss Crandall, that your establishment, falsely called a school, has been designed as the theater from which doctrines of amalgamation shall be promulgated as well as sentiments subverting the Union." He turned a page and read from his notes, "Pupils have been gathered from all quarters under the pretense of educating them, but really—here are the actual words—'to scatter firebrands, arrows and death among brethren of our own blood.'" He closed his notebook and looked at Prudence, expecting to hear a sharp retort from her lips.

She stared at him, then her gaze shifted to his sister Helen who stood beside him. She looked at Mr. Garrison, then at Samuel May. "I have no words," she said.

"Such proceedings disgrace an assembly of savage barbarians," Mr. Garrison remarked, almost at a loss for words himself.

"Prejudice to color does not surprise me," Samuel May spoke up, "but hostility to schools for making more intelligent citizens is a strange phenomenon, especially in this State which has always aimed to build up schools and protect women and children."

"Was any vote passed at the Meeting?"

"Yes, one that Andrew Judson as Clerk recorded." George Benson referred again to his notebook, "That a petition be made to the Legislature for a law against the bringing of colored people from other towns and states into Connecticut for any purpose."

"If a law is invoked to fight against you, Miss Crandall, we will secure law to fight for you," William Lloyd Garrison assured her. "During the struggle, public opinion will be aroused and that will prove to be our most powerful instrument."

"I know nothing of these matters, gentlemen, but I trust your understanding."

The clock on the mantel began to splutter a warning, then it struck the hour. Prudence glanced at Almira. "Six miles divides us, though nothing can our sentiments," she said, rising from her chair. "We must bid you good evening, friends, and return to our duties."

Almira rose and stood beside her sister.

"May a Sabbath peace pervade Canterbury tomorrow," Samuel May said in parting. "I shall drive over in the evening to meet your girls."

"There will be a cup of tea awaiting you," Almira promised.

"That expectation will shorten my journey, for I have heard from reliable sources that with Prudence Crandall, her tea is as excellent as her teaching."

Almira laughed gaily, but Prudence had little time for pleasantries. "It is our hope," she said, "that when we take the girls to church tomorrow and the people of the town see their decorum, that they will relent."

"It is well to hope," Mr. May's eyes were twinkling. "It is also well to remind yourself that people have a way of seeing what they want to see."

"Miss Crandall?"

"Yes, Mr. Benson?"

"Memory tells me that when the Committee for the Meeting House called on you in February you told them you would not bring your girls to Sunday attendance."

"Sir, I said I would not willingly give offense. Surely they cannot refuse us the right to worship tomorrow morning?"

Reverend Kneeland stepped forward. "If you find the doors of the church in Canterbury closed to you, Miss Crandall, those in Packerville will be open."

"I am grateful to you, sir, but I cannot believe that the people of Canterbury will draw a line of distinction in the matter of worship."

The sisters went down the path to the post where their horse had been tied. Climbing up to the seat of the wagon, Prudence took the reins and urged the horse along the road. "Mr. Kneeland is a kind man," she commented.

"And a zealous Abolitionist," Almira said. "I spent some time in converse with him."

"I had not noticed him particularly."

"Thee had no eyes for anyone but Mr. Garrison," Almira teased.

"Only because we both serve the same cause. Mr. Garrison is two years younger than I am, Sister," Prudence reminded Almira. "I have heard that he comes to Brooklyn not to see Samuel May alone but in the hope that Helen Benson will be present."

"Thee must be tired, Sister," Almira offered to take the reins in her hands.

Prudence shook her head. "Never have I felt in more excellent spirits."

Almira sighed dreamily. "I should like to be married to a man as genial as Samuel May, as lively as Mr. Garrison, and as apt to do a kindness as Mr. Kneeland."

"I shall never marry," Prudence said firmly.

"In many things thee knows best, Sister, but some things are taken away from us to decide."

"I am no longer young."

"Pff!" Almira exclaimed. "The right man would not think thirty too old, if he were older."

Doors Are Closed

Marcia stood at the window watching the people of Canterbury come from their houses and cross the Green to the Meeting House. It was a sunny morning. The sound of the church bell drawing people to worship filled the air. Prudence was ready to leave with her girls for church when the townspeople were in the building, safely ensconced in their pews and their prayers. She felt that her entrance at such a time could give no offense. From the schoolroom came the murmur of voices as Prudence talked with the girls.

"Please to take in your hands the book entitled *Guide to Good Manners* and open to page fifty-eight."

There was a fluttering of pages as the girls found their places.

"Beginning with Ann Eliza Hammond, I would have you read aloud by sentences and in turn, the paragraph entitled 'Deportment on the Sabbath.' The first sentence, if you please, Ann Eliza."

"'The Sabbath is designed as a day of rest from toil and for moral improvement,'" the girl read the words easily.

"'It should be observed as a day of thanksgiving,'" the next girl continued, "'for the cultivation of all that is amiable, noble and dignified in man.'"

"'A feeling of reverence should pervade the mind.'"

"'Neither long faces nor short faces are appropriate to the Sabbath, but a pleasing and dignified countenance is ever commendable.'"

"'It is a day in which to study the Bible, to cultivate the Christian graces, to learn our relation and duty to God, to ourselves, and to our fellow men.'"

"'It is—'"

Marcia left her post by the window and ran into the schoolroom. "You can leave now, Miss Prudence. It seems as if every one must be in church. The roads are empty."

"Thank you, Marcia, it is kind of you to stay and prepare our meal today. Follow me, girls. There is no need for haste. As long as the bell continues to toll, the doors will remain open. Hurry does not become a lady."

Marcia stood in the doorway and watched the two Miss Crandalls and their twelve scholars go down the walk, cross the road and approach the Meeting

House. Each girl carried a white handkerchief in one hand and a Bible in the other. They were all in their Sunday best, though that best was simplicity indeed, as Miss Prudence would not herself display or permit those in her charge to exhibit any extravagance of fashion. Plainness in dress was as much a rule of the school as was plainness of speech.

Some of the girls wore silk bonnets, some wore straw, but none bore trimming of any kind. Their frocks were sober in color and conformable in the size of sleeves, without bustles or flounces. A pin was allowed if it was required to hold a fichu in place, or a buckle if it was part of a belt; but nothing intended solely as ornament was to be worn. More than one dress made with an eye to elegance, rather than use, had been left in the bottom of a trunk to gather deeper folds.

Marcia's heart swelled with pride as she watched them cross the Green. Young as she was she felt a motherly concern for them all and she hoped they would go through the wide open doors before the bell in the steeple ceased ringing. Prudence, precise as always, had gauged things rightly, and Marcia saw that she was mounting the steps to the church porch as the last bell stroke echoed through the warm air. Marcia sighed happily and ran down the stairs to her kitchen to start making preparations for the noon meal.

It seemed only a matter of minutes before Marcia heard the front door open and close again. There was a patter of feet on the floor but no voices echoed in the passage. She came running up the stairs. Prudence and Almira stood silently while the girls filed past them into the schoolroom.

"Surely you were not late!" Marcia exclaimed.

"No, we were not late, Marcia."

"But—what happened?"

"Something I did not expect but which did not surprise me. We are unacceptable. The trustees of the building forbade us entrance and the doors were bolted against us."

Marcia looked bewildered. "What will you do now, Miss Prudence?"

"We shall worship in Packerville. Reverend Kneeland had promised us a welcome there, but I fear we shall have to wait until next Sunday."

"Packerville! That is two miles distant!"

"The miles do not matter, the welcome does. Almira, will thee join the girls and lead them in singing? Expect me presently. We shall worship under our own roof this morning, and this evening Samuel May will be with us to stir our hearts with noble sentiments."

"Yes, Sister."

Prudence turned to Marcia. "When you have finished your work, Marcia, I shall have a letter for you to carry to Mr. Kneeland in Packerville. On your way back, please to stop at my father's house and bring me news of him."

"Yes, Miss Prudence."

Long before twilight settled over the valley, bringing the day to its close, Samuel May arrived at the school. The girls greeted him shyly but respectfully, wondering what he would say to them; reserved in their response, they were scarcely ready for a sermon, after their experience of the morning.

Mr. May sat down with them in the parlor, urging them to draw their chairs closer to him. His brown eyes under their drooping lids were shining, and his mouth seemed more inclined to smile than to shape words. Always courteous in manner, he talked to the girls as if each one were a personal friend. Soon his neighborly tenderness enveloped them all. When Almira lit the lamp on the table, some of the girls looked at her in surprise. So much sunshine had come in with Mr. May that it was hard to believe dusk would soon fill the room.

"The girls and I shall be quite happy together," he said to Prudence, "and no doubt you have affairs of your own to attend to."

The sisters nodded to him and to each other, then left the group in the parlor and went into the schoolroom. Mr. May's voice, softly intoned but resonant from years of preaching, easily crossed the space between the two rooms.

"That is no sermon, Sister," Almira whispered.

Prudence shook her head. "He is telling them stories from his own boyhood. How they are listening! You cannot hear so much as the rustle of a skirt."

"I was about six years old then," Samuel May said

softly. "Running an errand for my mother, when a dog sprang after me—"

"Oh! oh!" little Maria Robinson exclaimed. "Were you badly frightened?"

"Indeed, yes! So much so that I kept looking backward as I ran away from him, then I tripped over a stone and struck my head on the ground. When I came to my senses, where should I be but in the arms of a large black woman who was saying soothingly to me, 'Don't be afraid, little boy. I know who you are. I'll carry you to your mama.'"

"Did she?"

"She did, and when she reached my home my mother cried out in alarm at the sight of me, for I was covered with blood. Mother took me in her arms to wash and dress the wound and only when that was done did she think to thank the kind woman who had brought me home. But my friend had disappeared. She wanted neither thanks nor reward, only to know that I was safe. My mother made many inquiries but, though we never found out who had been my benefactor, I have never failed to say thanks."

Emila Willson was puzzled. "How could you say thanks when you didn't have anyone to say them to?"

"There are many ways of saying thanks. Look for them and you'll find them."

"Tell us another story!"

"Please, Mr. May."

Prudence and Almira abandoned any pretense of

work and moved nearer the door to listen with the girls.

"I'll tell you a story about my grandmother," the cheery voice went on. "She was a gallant lady indeed and one night she was roused from her sleep by the appearance of a robber at her window. Springing from her bed she seized him by the shoulder and pushed him to the ground. 'You rascal,' she said to him, 'you'll wake my husband!'"

The girls laughed.

"Your grandmother wasn't afraid of anybody," Ann Eliza commented.

"Indeed, she was not! Once when she was asked what fear was she replied 'I don't know what the word means.'"

"Sister," Almira said quietly, "we should put the kettle over now and make preparations for tea. The girls can tell us next week in their compositions what we shall miss hearing."

Silently the sisters went through the passage and down the stairs to the kitchen. When they returned to join the girls, it was to see something different from the staid group that had first attended Samuel May. Two of the youngest were leaning against his knees. One girl was standing beside him with her arm resting on his shoulder, and the others had left their chairs and were sitting on the floor as close to him as they could get.

"I fear the girls are making too much of you, Mr.

May, for your own comfort," Prudence said apologetically.

"Ah, but I love to be muched!" he exclaimed.

Almira slipped her hand into her sister's and drew her toward the sofa. "Let decorum know a Sabbath," she whispered.

"Yes, it was a fine cat," Samuel May said, returning to his story.

"You mean that something happened to it?" one of the girls asked.

He nodded his head. "Only the other day that good woman and her daughter called on me carrying a basket covered with a clean white towel. I thought they had brought me a gift, but when I saw how sad they were I asked what the trouble was. They burst into tears and told me that some boys had set dogs on the cat and they had brought the cat's body to me for burial—" he paused.

"Did you have a funeral?"

"Yes, in my garden. They selected the spot between two currant bushes and I dug a deep safe grave. We spoke words of peace together and they left happier, knowing they had done all they could for their friend of many years. I was happy because I had done one of the duties for which a minister is ordained." Samuel May put his arms around the two who were leaning against his knees. The tone of his voice changed. Always tender, it carried with it an added firmness, as of one used to having commands obeyed.

"Sometimes what we can do is very little, but we must always do it."

Later that evening after the girls had gone to their rooms in Almira's charge, Prudence said to Samuel May, "Your words will live longer with the girls than any sermon they might have heard this morning."

"It is always in my mind to preach not what people wish to hear but what they need to hear." He smiled comfortingly at Prudence. "Your girls do not need to be challenged to put on strength so much as they need to be assured that kindness still lives in the world and that its expression has many forms."

"They have been here less than a week," Prudence went on, "but each one realizes that she has been called on to defend her right to education. The places of business in the town are closed to us. Now the church forbids us entrance. What more can be done?"

"The town may invoke the Vagrant Law."

"Surely that is obsolete now!"

"Perhaps, but being on the books it is enforceable."

"I scarcely know what it is."

"I have been familiarizing myself with local law since the Town Meeting and apparently the Select Men have the right to warn any person who is not an inhabitant of the town to depart. If the warning is not heeded, a fine of $1.67 for every week can be exacted."

Prudence laughed. "The town would soon have me in their debt since most of my scholars come from a distance."

"If the fine is not paid and the person warned does not depart after ten days, he or she shall be whipped on the naked body not exceeding ten stripes."

"That is barbarism!" Prudence exclaimed fervently.

"As our friend Garrison says, it is heathenism outdone. But you must not fear."

"I do not fear. Strangely enough fear has left me. Like your grandmother, I do not seem to know its smell or taste, but I must consider how to face the event of this law being invoked. Were I to pay the fine week after week, it would strain my already strained funds."

"You will be protected, Miss Crandall. There are many of us who feel your school must survive at any cost."

"I think," Prudence smiled, "I would like to survive with it."

Samuel May laughed heartily. "You shall, and the world will come to your defense."

"Sometimes, my friend, the pace of the world cannot match that of one small town, but I shall not hesitate or change my course. I have gone too far for that."

Samuel May rose from his chair. "I must be on my way back to Brooklyn. Bid your sister good night and let me urge you to call on me whenever I can act in your behalf. We must, as Mr. Garrison says, at all times show a brave front."

It was some time after Mr. May left that Marcia returned, hurrying up the stairs from the kitchen to present herself to the sisters sitting in the parlor.

"You need not whisper, Marcia. The girls went to bed an hour ago and must be asleep by now."

"Mr. Kneeland thanks you, Miss Prudence, for your letter and bids you welcome next Sunday. He says you have many friends in Packerville and that there are dealers there who will gladly furnish you with supplies."

"Oh, what good news!" Prudence sighed. "And my father, Marcia?"

"He wants you to know that Friends Meeting at Black Hill will always welcome you. He and Reuben will come with the wagon in good time on Sunday morning to take you all to Black Hill or Packerville, but—" Marcia paused.

"What is it, Marcia? You must not hesitate to speak freely."

"Your father asks, Miss Prudence, if you will not give up your school, sell your property, and relieve Canterbury of its imagined destruction."

"My father!" Prudence gasped. "But surely it was he who taught me to resist force but challenge wrong. As a child I often heard him say 'If a wrong has gone on forever, we Quakers think it has gone on long enough.' What can he mean? Why are you smiling, Marcia?"

"Please, Miss Prudence, he said he knew you would reply in such a fashion."

"Dear father, how I long for the sight of his face again!"

"He would have you know that he has been forbidden to see you, Miss Prudence."

"Father forbidden!" the sisters exclaimed.

Marcia nodded. "Today the constable called on him to say he must not come near you with water or supplies. He told your father it would be easy to raise a mob and tear down his house."

"What did Father say?"

"To me, Miss Prudence?" Marcia smiled widely. "He said to tell you that he would bring the hogshead of water tomorrow at the appointed time."

Prudence and Almira exchanged smiles.

"There is no authority that can enforce a law such as the constable voiced," Prudence said scornfully. "What do they hope to gain?"

"Intimidation, Sister," Almira suggested.

"Ha!" Prudence tossed her head as if to catch the breath of a high wind blowing. "They do not know of what stuff we Crandalls are made."

Before the month was out, the constable came to the school and presented Prudence Crandall with a warrant. Standing at the door, she read it calmly. The Vagrancy Law had been abused; the fine had not been paid; more than ten days had elapsed; the penalty must be exacted. The whipping was to take place on the Green that afternoon.

"Thank you," Prudence said icily. "This will be attended to at the proper time."

"But—" the constable began, only to find the door being closed in his face.

"Marcia," Prudence called, calmly, without emotion.

"Yes, Miss Prudence," Marcia's voice came up the stairs and was soon followed by her presence.

"Please drive to Brooklyn and urge Mr. May to come here with all speed."

Within three hours Samuel May had arrived, seeming more serene and cheerful than ever. "Have you told the girls what is to take place this afternoon?" he asked.

"Yes, I have told them, but when I told them something might happen at the last moment to hinder the event they were disappointed. All of them offered themselves eagerly to receive the ten stripes."

"Only one is needed."

"I know, and I have chosen Ann Eliza Hammond. She has great self-possession and dignity."

"May I speak with her?"

"Of course." Prudence went to the schoolroom and returned with Ann Eliza.

"So," Samuel May smiled at the girl, "you are the fortunate one!"

She returned his smile. "Sir, I count myself blest to have come to this day."

"I cannot believe that the Select Men of the town will actually attempt to inflict this punishment, but should they—can you bear it?"

Ann Eliza considered a moment.

"I cannot say that I will not flinch, Mr. May, but that I will not cry out I can promise."

"Ten stripes they wish to exact, no more, no less. Should they do this, those stripes will resound not on your bare back alone but on the whole civilized world. There will be such an expression of indignation that it will make Mr. Judson and his associates quail."

Early in the afternoon the constable, supported by three of the Select Men, came to Prudence Crandall's door, writ in hand. Marcia conducted them to the parlor where they faced Samuel May. On either side of him stood the sisters, both resolved and calm. Ann Eliza stood quietly near the window. The atmosphere of the room was such a peaceful one that it exasperated the constable and in his confusion he handed the writ first to Samuel May, then seized it abruptly and waved it in Prudence's face, demanding that she comply with the law.

"Willingly," she replied.

"Mr. Constable," Samuel May began, "this young girl is quite ready to receive the penalty *if* the Vagrant Law has been abused. We ask to accompany her, for decency's sake."

"With malice and intent, Prudence Crandall has broken the law," the constable answered gruffly.

"If I have read your law correctly," Mr. May said, "it is not broken if maintenance is guaranteed those scholars from beyond the borders of Connecticut."

"That's the way it reads," the constable agreed.

"Then, gentlemen," Mr. May smiled, "you may as well return to your worthy occupations, for Miss Crandall's scholars are all protected by bond."

Prudence drew in her breath sharply. A cry of joy escaped Almira, and both turned to face Samuel May; but he had already started toward the door, his arm linked in that of the constable's.

"Your visit, gentlemen, is interfering with the work of the school," he was saying to them. "Please leave with all diligence and as quietly as you can."

No persuasion of his could dim the anger in the voices of the Select Men as, arguing among themselves, they left the school. When Mr. May returned to the parlor, Prudence ran toward him.

"What have you done, Samuel May, to give us such relief and our enemies such discomfort?"

"An hour ago I posted a bond with the Canterbury Town Treasurer," he explained, with an air that was almost jaunty. "It was signed by myself and leading men in Brooklyn. The Select Men and the constable will see it when they return to their office."

"Will that satisfy them?" Almira asked.

"It should, dear lady, for a time at least. The bond was in the amount of $10,000."

Prudence gasped.

Ann Eliza came forward. "So you will not need me now?" Disappointment was in her voice.

"No, child, you may return to your school work."

The girl started to speak, then went slowly from the room.

"What will they do next?" Prudence asked.

"Who can tell? An old law has proved worthless, but they are already trying to frame a new one. Certain men of the town, headed by Andrew Judson, are circulating a petition to be laid before the General Assembly, urging it to enact a law to prevent the establishment of such schools as yours."

Prudence sighed with relief. "State Legislatures move slowly. We shall have peace for awhile to go on with our work."

"Do not count too much on an interim," Samuel May warned. "While the men in authority wait for legal power they may not hesitate to make your life uncomfortable."

That night, after the girls were asleep and only one lamp remained alight in the house, Prudence and Almira talked together in their bedroom.

"It is late, Sister, and thee should have rest," Almira said tenderly.

"I think I am too tired to sleep," Prudence replied.

"Thee would rest better without shoes and dress."

Prudence stood up, wanting to please her sister though she felt sapped of strength. It was an effort to take off her clothes and her fingers moved laggardly with hooks and laces. When she bent down to unbutton her shoes a blinding pain seized her. She let out a sudden cry and, putting her hands to her head, rocked silently back and forth.

Almira flew across the room and flung her arms around Prudence. "Sister, what is the matter?"

"I feel—" Prudence fought against the faintness engulfing her, "—strangely unwell. Help me to bed, Sister."

Almira steadied her across the room until they reached the bed, then she helped Prudence undress and put on a flannel nightgown. With nimble fingers she rubbed the hands and feet that were so cold. After a few moments she went to the wash basin and wrung water from a cloth which she laid on Prudence's brow.

"When thee feels better, Sister, I will run across the road to fetch Dr. Harris."

"No, no, Almira, it is too late. Tomorrow, if I am not quite well, you may call him but I would not disturb him now. It is nothing. A sip of linden tea may help me to sleep."

Almira hastened from the room to get the tea, trying to calm, in her own mind, dire thoughts and a tumult of anger against the town that was making her sister's way so difficult.

By morning Prudence felt no better. A great weakness had assailed her and the throbbing of her head seemed deeper than hot or cold cloths could reach. She was willing to have Almira fetch the doctor. "Tell him I feel dolorous indeed," she said wearily.

Almira, throwing a cloak over her shoulders, ran across the road to the Harris' house. She knocked repeatedly on the door until it was opened by the doctor's wife who looked at her strangely.

"Good morning, Mrs. Harris, I pray that I have not disturbed you unduly. Is the doctor—"

The door was closing again.

"He cannot see you," Mrs. Harris was saying.

"Oh, but I must see him! It is urgent, very urgent." Almira's heart was in her voice and eyes. Something of it touched Mrs. Harris before the door had closed entirely.

"Wait a moment and I'll speak with him. No, not inside, on the step."

Almira stood waiting, but it was all of ten minutes before Mrs. Harris returned. "He says he cannot see you."

"But my sister is very ill."

"If she were dying he could not see her. Or you. Or any of the girls in the school."

"Not—see her?"

Mrs. Harris shook her head.

"But—but why?" Almira's throat had constricted so with horror that she could scarcely speak the words.

"He has been forbidden to attend anyone in Miss Crandall's house."

"Forbidden! By whom?"

"By Mr.—" Mrs. Harris hesitated, "by the men in authority in Canterbury."

Almira looked around her desperately. "Who will help us?"

"There is a doctor in Plainfield."

"That is a long way to go if the need be sudden. What if anything should happen to one of the girls? They are in our care while with us—"

The door that had been closing as Almira was speaking was now firmly shut. She stared at the unfeeling wooden panels and raised her hands to beat on them again. Then she dropped her hands and turned away with a heavy heart and eyes clouded by tears. Longing as she was to save Prudence this added burden, she knew there was only one thing to do and that was go straight to Prudence's bedside and tell her what had taken place. Almira walked slowly across the road. She wanted to have command of her voice and be able to look Prudence in the eyes when she spoke to her. Prudence was brave and she expected everyone else to be brave too, but she did not remember that all were not made of the same stuff.

Prudence listened while Almira told her the result of her call on the doctor. "We must live wisely and well while the girls are in our care so sickness cannot visit them," she replied, "and we must study how to care for them in accident. Breaks. Burns. Such things can happen in any household, and we must know how to deal with them. Reuben will help us. He has made a study of medicine."

"But thee, sister dear, it is thee I want to see well."

Prudence raised her head on the pillow. "I shall get well, Almira, with the help of God and not the doctor, and once I am well, I shall be stronger than ever."

Law Is Enforced

The days wore on and serenity reigned within the school. The girls, their number now increased to seventeen, worked well, rallying against persecution with a sense of glory. Prudence and Almira, inspiring them with courage, made each one feel that what happened outside was not directed to her personally but to her race.

Unpleasantness cheerfully endured was a victory for all Negroes, just as lessons mastered was a proof of their ability. Friends and families often came to visit and though all traffic with the stages had been forbidden anyone connected with the school, a friendly Negro in Norwich put his conveyances at Miss Crandall's disposal and did whatever transporting was required.

Injustice spread no gloom within the walls of the school, for the girls were bound in a circle of sisterly affection, and when they walked abroad in the afternoons they disregarded the catcalls and hooting horns that followed them. Sometimes, on their walks, Prudence encountered one or another of her former pupils. Glad words came to her lips, but invariably the girls would turn hastily away, averting their eyes or hiding their faces behind quickly opened fans. Such behavior from those whom she had grown to love while she was their teacher hurt Prudence more than the mischief their brothers devised. She could forgive the girls because of their youth; it was not so easy to forgive their fathers.

As the May days brought greening growth to fields and gardens, the people of Canterbury became too busy with their own concerns to molest the school. Often a day, sometimes a whole succession of days, passed without an incident, but Prudence was not to be thrown off her guard. "There is ever calm before a storm," she warned her scholars, "and until we hear what the Legislature decides we will be prepared for anything."

So the lessons went on—spelling, geography, arithmetic; yet none more important than manners and sewing.

"We have now reached Lesson XXXVI in English Composition," Prudence announced one morning. "The subject before us is that of Simple Themes and I would have you all ponder well the first lines of our lesson. Your books are open? Very well." She held her book up and read to the listening group, "'Before taking up the pen to write, it will be well to think for some time on the subject'—yes, Marcia?" She turned her gaze to the girl who had entered the room.

"Please, Miss Prudence, your father wishes to have a word with you."

A look of surprise passed over Prudence's face. "I shall be with him shortly, Marcia." She returned her attention to the girls. "Our lesson deals with the comparison between History and Biography." Again she read from the book, "'Both history and biography teach philosophy by example, but the example exhibited by biography is the more interesting.' Sarah Harris, please to read the next sentence."

Sarah rose and stood by her desk, book in hand. "'The single character of biography engages more of our attention than it would do if mixed with others equally conspicuous.'"

"Anne Peterson, read the next, please."

"'We form, as it were, a friendship for a single character in biography, and our benevolent affections are the stronger for being fixed upon one.'"

"Now, let us all read together the concluding sentence, 'Universal benevolence sounds prettily, but it is particular benevolence only that proves our moral character.'" Prudence closed her book. "You may devote the rest of the hour to composing a biography, but remember to think before you write."

She went from the room and ran swiftly down the stairs to greet Pardon Crandall who was waiting for her in the kitchen.

"Father," she cried joyously, "surely it must be good news that brings thee here at such an hour! Has the General Assembly paid heed at last to the letter thee sent them?"

"No, daughter, it is indeed quite the opposite."

"So!" Prudence exclaimed, and her expression became serious.

"I implored them to remember the truth that all men are created equal and not to pass any act that would destroy the rights of the people of this State, whatever their color; but they have chosen to forget. Their reply comes by means of a letter in Andrew Judson's hand."

"Let me see it, please."

Pardon reached into his pocket and handed his daughter a letter.

Prudence took it, reading aloud words that had no longer any power to shock or anger, only to sadden, "—your printed paper—did not injure us; it helped— in getting the bill through. When they received it every man clenched his fists, and the chairman of the committee sat down and doubled the penalty. Members of the Legislature said to me, 'If this law does not answer your purpose, let us know, and next year we will make you one that will.'"

Prudence put her arms around her father's neck as she had when a child and, overcome by tears, she spent her sorrow against his strength; but there were no tears in her eyes now.

"Perhaps I did thee harm, daughter, when I sent my paper to the Assembly."

"No, no, dear Father, thee did but confirm my stand. Who gave thee this letter?"

"Two members of the Civil Authority, telling me at the same time that if I came to see thee I would be fined $100 for the first offense and $200 for the second, with the amount ever doubling." Pardon shrugged his shoulders. "The fine holds for anyone coming to see thee."

"And so thee came!" She stood away from him to look into his eyes, searching for the valor his quiet words veiled.

"Yes, I came also to warn thee that since the law has been passed they intend to show no mercy. The Civil Authority told me that if thee did not yield, thee would be taken up the same way as for stealing a horse, or burglary. Property will not be taken, but thee will be put in jail."

"Since they have passed a law, they may indeed do all they say," Prudence commented.

"This is the twenty-fourth day of May, the sun is shining and I have a field to plough," Pardon Crandall said. "Reuben went fishing early this morning. He will soon be bringing thee some trout."

"In spite of the fine!"

"A fine means no more to Reuben than the passing of a law to thee." Pardon smiled with honest pride. "Good day, daughter."

The day might have passed into evening peacefully had not the stillness of the town been suddenly shattered by the ringing of the church bell and the firing of a cannon from a nearby hill.

"What has happened, Miss Prudence?"

"What great thing has happened?" the girls asked, looking from the windows of the house at the people of Canterbury as they gathered in jubilant groups outside places of business and beside their front gates, talking excitedly together.

"You would think a battle had been won!"

"May we go out, Miss Prudence, and discover the cause of such rejoicing?"

"No, girls. We will know soon enough. It is time for you to prepare your work for tomorrow."

Reluctantly the girls left her and went to the schoolroom, but the constant booming of the cannon and sounding of the church bell made concentration difficult.

"What can it mean, Sister?" Almira asked.

"It is the sound of joy, Almira, but something within tells me that the joy does not embrace us."

Charles Harris came that evening to see Marcia, but he had news for Miss Crandall. Marcia brought him to the parlor where the sisters were bent over their sewing, mending garments and renewing household linen.

"Miss Crandall," he said impulsively, "I had hoped to reach you before the news became known by the town, but it has taken me longer than I expected to get to Canterbury. The roads are crowded and people everywhere in the county seem bent on celebration."

An odd look crossed Prudence's face. "I had never thought to be the means of widespread merriment."

"You know, then, what it is all about?"

"I have a surmise, Charles. Earlier in the day my father informed me of the law passed by the Legislature. I trust that you have with you a copy of the law?"

"Yes, I have." He reached into his pocket. "I am on my way to Boston to place it on *The Liberator*'s desk."

Prudence took it from him and started to read. "This concerns us all," she said quietly, reading aloud in a voice as composed as if it were a lesson being given her scholars.

Almira left her chair to stand beside her sister, one arm around her. Charles and Marcia stood side by side. From the rooms above, where the girls were preparing for bed, there was the sound of murmuring voices, mingled with laughter rising into song and the patter of slippered feet as some of the younger ones played games.

"'Section One. Be it enacted by the Senate and House of Representatives, in General Assembly convened, that no person shall set up or establish in this State any school, academy, or literary institution for the instruction or education of colored persons who are not inhabitants of this State.'" The sound of Prudence Crandall's voice was low and controlled, but her hands tightened on the paper as she went on, "'Nor instruct or teach in any school, or other literary institution whatsoever, in this State; nor harbor or board, for the purpose of attending or being taught or instructed in any such school, academy, or literary institution, any colored person who is not an inhabitant of any town in this State, without the consent in writing, first obtained, of a majority of the Civil Authority, and also of the Select Men of the town, in which such school, academy, or literary institution is situated—'"

Prudence stopped reading. She closed her eyes for a moment as if to make the silence of the room her own, then she handed the paper back to Charles Harris.

He took it from her and returned it to his pocket. "So your school must be closed," he said quietly. "Mr. Garrison will be sorry when he hears this. He had hoped—"

Prudence flashed stern eyes at him. "The school will not be closed! I intend to renew my advertisement in *The Liberator*. We have seventeen girls now and there is room for that many more."

"Miss Crandall, the penalty for violation of the law is severe."

"Indeed?"

"It is imprisonment."

Prudence laughed sharply. "I have yet to see the indignity I cannot bear. Charles, please to carry my respects to *The Liberator* since Mr. Garrison is in England and cannot receive them in person. Tell all that we are in good health and the school is flourishing. Marcia, see that Charles has something substantial to eat before he goes on his way. Come, Almira, the girls have had their diversion long enough."

A transient peace followed the Legislature's decision, as if the people having secured the law were willing to wait for its ponderous machinery to act.

"It is an infamous law and it will surely be repealed," George Benson said one evening, when he and Samuel May sat at the Crandall sisters' tea table.

"It will," Samuel May agreed, "but not in time to help our friend, Prudence. Fifty years from now this Black Law of Connecticut may be as great a source of amusement as some of her Blue Laws are to us now."

"I wonder how many of us will be here then," Almira murmured as she cut generous pieces from a cake of her own baking.

"I am sure you will, Almira, and Prudence too. May you both reap a rich harvest from the seed you are sowing."

Inclining their heads slightly, the sisters accepted Mr. May's gallantry; then his tone became more serious, "I fear that it will take years and much education for the Legislators to undo what they have just done."

"Show me the evil that cannot be turned to some good," Prudence remarked.

"That is what we all feel strongly." Samuel May turned toward her eagerly. "If you can face the penalty of the law you will do a great service."

"I shall be sentenced when I am brought to trial on the twenty-seventh day of June," Prudence said.

"You can be spared the unpleasantness of imprisonment if you will allow your friends to post bail."

"That is an easy way out!" Prudence exclaimed, the tone of her voice scornful.

"True. The hard way will draw attention to you and the Cause."

"I have no liking for attention, but I will yield to anything that will promote the Cause. Put me in the hands of those with whom the law originated and its hideous features will be shown."

George Benson was smiling. "We hoped you would feel that way, Miss Crandall."

"Indeed, dear Prudence," Samuel May beamed at her, "you are a daughter of the Gospel, finding joy in bonds."

"I cannot accept your flattery." She shook her head. "I know full well that I shall find no joy in the bonds, only in what they exhibit. Now, gentlemen, you must have another piece of Almira's cake."

"Since you are willing to accept the penalty, I will call on all your supporters and counsel them to give no bonds in your behalf."

"It is a grievous thing you ask of my sister," Almira said quietly as she passed the cake.

"But it will not last long," Samuel May replied, "and nothing will expose to the public the virulence of the law and the malice of the persecution as the fact that Prudence Crandall has been thrust into jail."

Prudence reached toward Mr. May's tea cup. "Let me fill your cup again."

"Not to the full, a half will do."

She smiled as she poured the tea, filling the cup full. "I can still hear my grandmother saying 'Never break a cup.'"

He lifted it to his lips. "In tea, as well as in matters of law, you are willing to go all the way."

"I am indeed."

Before the visitors left, Samuel assured Prudence that he would make all the arrangements that were practicable for her comfort while in prison.

"If they will allow you a companion," George Benson added, "my sister Mary will ask for the honor of staying with you."

"Tell her that the prospect of her company fills me with even greater anticipation," Prudence replied.

On the morning of the twenty-seventh of June, Prudence stood by her window looking out across the Green. Two hours earlier she had watched the sun rise at one side of the Meeting House; now it was moving on into a cloudless sky on the other side of the stately white building. Her day was often marked by the position of the sun and she liked to watch it set behind the low hills in the west, but this was one day when the sun would not set for her in Canterbury. Two men were crossing the Green in the direction of her house. One she recognized at a distance as the constable, but even lessening distance brought no recognition of the other. However, she did not need to be told that he was the sheriff. Their mission she knew.

When they crossed the road and reached her gate, she went down the stairs to meet them. The night before she had said good-by to her girls, promising them she would not be long away from them and commending them to Almira. She had told Marcia that she would attend the door, for she wanted to leave the school quietly and with no show of emotion.

"Good morning, gentlemen," she said, standing in the doorway. "I am quite ready to go with you. May I ask that one of you carry my bag?"

"What's it for?" the sheriff asked, looking at her suspiciously.

"I assure you that it contains neither firebrands nor arrows," Prudence said, "but a few articles of feminine apparel whose sight might cause you embarrassment."

"You won't be needing that." The constable pushed the bag with his foot away from the door.

"Permit me to know my own needs," Prudence replied. "I ask that you make no further disturbance.

My scholars are at work. Come, let us go." She drew the door to behind her and started down the walk.

The sheriff picked up the bag and carried it. Prudence waited for the two men at the gate, then, with the sheriff on one side and the constable on the other, they crossed the road and walked over the Green to the Meeting House where the Civil Authority and Select Men had gathered.

Rufus Adams and Asael Bacon, acting as judges of the local court, were impatient to examine their prisoner and accept the bonds she was sure to offer. It was not to their liking to sentence a woman to prison, no matter how much they disagreed with her. With little formality, Mr. Adams informed Prudence that she had not only violated but was continuing daily to violate a statute law of the State of Connecticut.

"Of that I am fully aware."

"You are committed to trial at the next session of the Supreme Court in Brooklyn, in August."

"I shall be present."

"Your word is not sufficient," Mr. Bacon interjected hastily. "Bonds must be posted during the intervening weeks to guarantee your presence."

Prudence made no reply.

"If bonds are not posted." Mr. Adams continued, "you—er, you face imprisonment."

"I am prepared to receive the full penalty of the law."

"Perhaps you do not understand, Miss Crandall." Rufus Adams leaned toward her. "There is no need for you to go to jail if your friends are willing to post bonds for you."

"Surely, you have some friends?" Mr. Bacon asked.

"My school has many patrons, I myself have many supporters, but I do not choose to ask them to pledge surety for me."

"Fine friends they must be not to come to your rescue!" Mr. Bacon exclaimed.

"You have expressed my feelings, Mr. Bacon. They are good friends, indeed. Gentlemen, may I ask you to proceed with your duty?"

Mr. Adams looked at her seriously. "Miss Crandall, will you consider what you are saying. Otherwise, the necessity you force us to is disagreeable in the extreme."

"To you, gentlemen, or to me?"

Asael Bacon sighed with exasperation, then he looked around the room.

"Is there no one to speak in the prisoner's defence?" he asked.

The stalwart faces of the men who represented the Civil Authority in Canterbury looked back at him. The Select Men set their lips and shook their heads. In their hearts they might want to save their town the disgrace of sending a woman to jail, but in the device of a law they had helped frame, they were powerless. Silence filled the room.

Rufus Adams conferred with Asael Bacon, then he turned to the constable. "Take Prudence Crandall to

Brooklyn and put her in the hands of the jailer there. She is a felon and even her femininity will not save her from a felon's fate." He coughed and turned back to Mr. Bacon, but his fellow judge indicated that he was the one to speak.

"Miss Crandall," Mr. Adams faced his prisoner, "to assure you of our leniency, we will send a messenger to certain of your friends and request them to put up the required bail."

"I think you will find none of them at home, Mr. Adams."

"But surely you—"

"Mr. Adams, it is not for me you would do this, but to save yourselves. Thank you, gentlemen, but I have chosen the way in which I must walk. I ask that you conduct me with reasonable dispatch to my destination."

The drive from Canterbury to Brooklyn in the spring wagon, behind a pair of strong grays, was a pleasant one. The sheriff held the reins and Prudence sat between him and the constable. Few words were exchanged during the six mile journey, but Prudence felt keenly aware of the blessing of silence. Haymaking had commenced. The fields were filled with laborers and the air with fragrance.

Prudence breathed deeply. Farmer's daughter as she was, she savored the drying grass and its promise of winter food. Low round hills crowned with stands of chestnut and oak, upland farms where crops grew strong from good brown soil, wide pastures watered by streams—all seemed brooded over by a dreaming peace. Passing a house that stood near the road, Prudence noticed how lush the gooseberries were on the bushes, how red the clusters of currants. Around the doorway a trumpet vine made a luxurious frame. The year was at its height and its yield would be abundant.

As the wagon drew up to the jail and the grays came to a halt, Samuel May, who had been waiting there, came forward. Prudence got down from the wagon and looked at him questioningly. In their brief moment of greeting, Samuel saw her not as the fighter in a great cause but what she was in herself, and he became alarmed at what he and other Abolitionists were asking her to do. When the constable had gone off with the horses and the sheriff had preceded them into the jail, he turned to her.

"If you feel hesitant, Prudence," he whispered, "if you dread this gloomy place and wish to be saved from it, I will post the bonds for you now. I have them in my pocket."

"Oh, no," she replied, while the zest in her voice said more than any words for the feeling within her. "I am only afraid that they will not put me in jail!"

Together they walked through the open door.

"The room in which you are to be confined is, unfortunately, the one in which Oliver Watkins spent his last night on earth."

"That was two years and more ago. I trust the winds have blown through it since then! Poor man, I remember well the day of his hanging. It was said that people came from far and near to see it, and as they ran past his window he called to them and told them not to hurry, that nothing could happen until he got there."

"It is the best room they have, Prudence, and the jailor has put it in nice order. George Benson and I have brought a bedstead and fresh bedding from our homes, and Mary Benson will soon be here to spend the night with you."

"I scarcely deserve such kindness."

"Everyone is entitled as much to courtesy as to justice," Samuel May said.

They went into the room where several people had gathered and the sheriff was sitting at a long table, but as he seemed to be busy with every matter except theirs, they sat down on a bench to await his pleasure.

"I wish he would not delay so," Prudence murmured.

Two men standing near approached Samuel May and addressed him reproachfully. "It is a disgrace to our State, sir, to imprison this woman."

"I agree with you heartily and you may prevent it if you care to do so."

"Oh, we are no friends of hers, and we are not in favor of her school," one of the men said.

The other shook his fist in Mr. May's face. "You

Abolitionists who have encouraged her, should not desert her now."

"That we do not intend to do."

"Why do you allow her to face this indignity?"

"To prove that the law recently enacted is an evil one." Samuel May smiled disarmingly at the young men. "My good friends, it is the people now who must change the law and they will do so when they see how cruel it is, but that they will not see unless we allow its full penalties to be inflicted."

Prudence listened quietly, shifting on the bench occasionally and glancing from time to time at the sheriff.

"Don't you mind what they are making you do?" one of the young men turned to her.

"I am willing to bear anything for the Cause," she replied, "but this delay wearies me."

An hour later the sheriff left his various affairs and went up to Prudence. "Come along now," he said gruffly, "it's getting late and I want to be home by nightfall." He led the way and gestured her to follow him.

Prudence moved slowly. Samuel May, walking beside her, assured her there was no need to hurry. At the end of the passage they met the jailor, keys in hand.

"You're in his hands now," the sheriff said, turning abruptly as if he wanted to put the matter away from him.

The jailor led them to a cell. He turned one of his keys in the lock and pushed back the heavy bolt.

"There you are," he said, "and it's as nice a room as you could find any place."

Prudence walked in. The room was small and twilight had already begun to fill it. The single window was criss-crossed with bars, the door was stoutly reinforced. Half-way across the room she turned around and faced Samuel May who had set her bag inside the door. "How long must I remain here?"

"Until you're tried," the jailor answered.

Samuel shook his head. "No, no, she has friends who will give the required bonds. Tomorrow morning, Prudence, you will be released. You will not be long alone for Mary will soon be here."

"Oh, I do not mind being alone, but I would like to return to my work as soon as possible."

"You are doing it equally here."

"Thank you," Prudence smiled faintly, "for reminding me of that."

"Time's up." The jailor jangled his keys.

Prudence stood still in the center of the room, her head framed by the bars at the window and the fading light of day.

The door swung to. The bolts moved into place. The key turned in the lock.

"She seems a nice-appearing lady," the jailor remarked. "What's she done to get herself into this place?"

"She opened a school for girls of color."

The jailor shook his head wearily. "Seems as if

every day they find more ways people can do wrong. Who would have thought that was a crime?" He tested the door to make sure it was fast. "Come along." He started down the passage.

"The deed is done and it cannot be recalled," Samuel May said as he looked back at the door that was locked and barred. "Now it has passed into the history of our nation and our age." He hastened along the passage, his footsteps resounding through the hollow silence.

First Trial

It was the morning of August twenty-second. Pardon Crandall stood in the kitchen talking with his daughters. "Thee has gone far, Prudence, but I begin to fear thee is going too far."

"For what, Father?"

"Content. Peace."

"Oh," she raised her head, "I do not think of such things. I pray for strength to continue on to the end of my task."

"There are great issues at stake, daughter. No longer is the question one of the right to teach a few girls, but one of whether our nation will respect the rights of all men. Sometimes I think thee is like a small nut in a cracker." He sighed wearily, conscious of his failing powers at a time when his daughter needed all the support he could give her.

Almira put her arm through her father's and walked with him to the settle. "Rest yourself, dear Father," she said gently.

He touched her hand with his, cheered by her tenderness. The strain and anxiety of the past months had told on him and his once rugged frame seemed bent under a load of care.

"Prudence is strong, Father, she will endure."

"And triumph, too!" Prudence exclaimed.

"I would not have thee spend another night in jail, daughter."

"Great good was accomplished by that one night, Father. People were shocked, public opinion was aroused, and sympathy for the Cause strengthened. Indeed, they say that nothing has operated so effectually as the establishment of my school to bring the claims of the colored population before the public."

Pardon shook his head; such talk was too close to pride to please him.

"My friends can now be numbered in their hundreds, Father, and letters of encouragement arrive daily."

Almira ran across the room to put her hands on a recent copy of *The Liberator*. "See, dear Father, this letter that tells of a concert of prayer in our Prudence's behalf! Here is a correspondent who asks all her feminine friends who desire the success of the school to set apart a short time every day to pray in secret that the blessing of God rest on Prudence."

Pardon smiled, and with the smile, some of the weariness seemed to leave his face. "Almost my two daughters persuade me that they thrive on struggle as a pair of goats on stony soil."

"Have no fear, Father," Prudence said, "the Cause cannot fail."

"The Cause cannot, daughter, for it has time on its side, but thee, with only a mortal's span of time and energy, may. I like not the looks of those arrayed against thee in this trial—Jonathan Welch, Ichabod Bulkeley and Andrew Judson."

"But, Father, Arthur Tappan has assured Samuel of his generous support and three of the ablest lawyers have been secured in my defense—Calvin Goddard, Henry Strong and Mr. W. W. Ellsworth."

Pardon repeated the names. "They are all good men and distinguished members of the Connecticut Bar, but I doubt if their ability can outstrip the adroitness of those in league against thee."

"My counsel is convinced that the Black Law is unconstitutional and will be pronounced so by this Court," Prudence said stoutly, "or by a higher one, if the case must be carried on," she added.

"Ah," Pardon looked quickly at his daughter, "so thee does not feel certain that this trial may settle everything?" Eagerness animated him and his eyes flashed with something of the fire seen in his daughter's.

Prudence shook her head.

"That is all I need to know, daughter." Pardon rose from his seat and went toward her. "I did not want thee to count too much on immediate success."

"The sound of that word is sweet," Prudence said. "Perhaps I shall hear it sometime." She leaned toward her father and kissed him impulsively.

Pardon looked into her face, meeting the strong unwavering gaze of her eyes. "My heart has ached for thee, daughter. I have not much longer to live and have little to lose. Life is still before thee."

"Life would mean nothing to me, Father, if I lived it against my conscience."

Steps could be heard outside and the sound of voices. Almira got up and ran to the window. She turned quickly to face her sister. "They have come for thee, Prudence."

Prudence kissed her father again, then she looked at Almira. "Comfort each other in my absence. No, do not come to the door. I shall return in good time and—" she lifted her head, "the school will go on."

Pardon and Almira watched her leave the room. They listened to her footsteps on the stairs.

"She is in the schoolroom talking to the girls," Almira whispered.

Then her footsteps could be heard in the passage. There was the sound of the front door opening, a murmur of voices, and the door closing again. Soon, only the wheels of a carriage on the road and the clopping of hooves could be heard. The house seemed empty and as lonely as if it had been abandoned of all life, though there were sounds in the schoolroom above and Almira and Pardon still faced each other.

"She moves into greatness, Father."

"I would have had her move into happiness, but we cannot choose."

The Courtroom in Brooklyn was hot that August morning when Prudence Crandall walked calmly in and took her place in the stand. She bowed to Judge Eaton who was presiding and to her three lawyers; she looked at the jury, her keen blue eyes resting on one after another of the twelve men; she acknowledged the presence of Mr. Judson and his colleagues, then she sat down and loosened the ribbons that held her bonnet in place. She settled herself into her chair, smoothed the folds of her dress, and took a small fan from her reticule. A long time might elapse before she would be allowed to leave and she wished to have everything ready for reasonable comfort.

Judge Eaton raised his gavel and brought it down on the desk. The sound put an end to all whisperings and movements. Silence came over the Courtroom and everyone present turned to face Judge Eaton as he stated the case of Prudence Crandall versus the State of Connecticut, then indicated that the prosecution might proceed.

Andrew Judson rose from his seat. He glanced casually around the room, then turned to the Jury as if the twelve men there were the only ones present. In a voice that flamed with conviction, he commenced his remarks. "Gentlemen of the Jury—"

Prudence saw by the papers in his hand that what he had to say could not be said under a long time. The three men who were to speak in her defense were listening keenly, but there seemed little need for her to follow Mr. Judson's remarks as she knew his argument well and his words only disturbed the tenor of her mind. She turned her gaze away from him and let it rest lightly on one face after another of the people in the Courtroom.

Many had come out of curiosity; some had come in malice. The expressions on their faces as they followed Mr. Judson's remarks spoke clearly of what was in their minds. But others were there for her support and encouragement. Prudence found herself smiling inwardly as she let her gaze rest on their faces, whether they were known to her or not.

Samuel May was following every word, but his face was serene as ever, and from it Prudence drew a cheerful courage. Next to him sat George Benson, taking notes for *The Liberator,* and Charles Burleigh making notes for *The Unionist*. William Burleigh was at his brother's left and the two exchanged glances frequently. The sight of them both made Prudence feel comfortable, for William was now teaching in her school and Charles was editing the paper which had been founded expressly to defend her and give the school publicity.

Prudence recalled with what excitement she had read the first issue only a month ago. For some months previously, Samuel May had endeavored to persuade the editors of various papers to report news of the school, but without exception they had told him it would be the end of their papers if they did. Then, when Arthur Tappan had signified his interest in the school and devoted the sum of $10,000 to its defense, both he and Samuel May had felt it imperative that a paper be issued and circulated widely through State and nation to share the struggle with *The Liberator.* So *The Unionist* had been founded and Charles Burleigh chosen to edit it. Prudence's eyes searched the room for Arthur Tappan.

"He must be attending to his business in New York," she said to herself. She had met him only once when he visited her school shortly after the passing of the Black Law, but she had been deeply impressed that the wealthy silk merchant, whose name was synonymous with philanthropy, felt such concern for her work. He had seen further ahead than she how long and costly her battle with the Courts might be, and he had told Mr. May to consider him his banker and to spare no expense that the case might be thoroughly tried.

"How can one man do so much?" Prudence had

asked Samuel May, when they stood watching the stage coach depart on its way to New York, with Arthur Tappan among its passengers.

"He commands time as he does money and is able to sponsor reforms and patronize philanthropies with the greatest of ease."

"But how?" Prudence had pressed.

Samuel had smiled. "Have you never heard of the rules he adopted early in his business career?"

She had shaken her head.

"He vowed never to have a chair in his office for visitors and always to place a fixed price and that as low as possible on all his goods."

Prudence put her fan up to her face to hide the smile that crept across it at the thought of Arthur Tappan. Then she moved the fan slowly to stir the sultry air and brought her mind back with difficulty to the Courtroom.

Andrew Judson's voice rumbled on. Words and phrases hung for a moment in the air and held her attention, "—keep out of the State injurious kind of population—could enjoy advantages of district schools—South free slaves—send all to Connecticut . . ."

Prudence sighed inwardly and looked out again to draw comfort from the presence of her supporters. Reverend Kneeland from Packerville was sitting near Samuel May. His eyes were on Mr. Judson and his hands, clenched in his lap, seemed to tighten visibly as the argument went on.

"He looks tired," Prudence thought. She was not surprised, for Levi Kneeland's sympathies were wide and he entered heart and soul into whatever stirred them. Earnest and hard-working, he labored with such intensity, that his life might count for nothing against the question of the moment. Prudence, her eyes on him, felt alarmed when she saw what must have been a twinge of pain seize his body and pass over his face. His eyes closed and his hands ground themselves together. The man sitting beside Levi Kneeland was aware of something, for he bent his head and whispered a few words to him. Mr. Kneeland shook his head and leaned back in his chair, as if the other man's concern had relaxed an inner tightness.

Prudence turned her attention to the man sitting next to the Baptist minister. He was a stranger to her, but to all appearances he was one of her supporters. He was a strongly built man and she thought that he must stand tall. He was older than Samuel May or Levi Kneeland, for what there was of dark auburn hair was liberally streaked with gray. "But not much older," she told herself, "I doubt if he is fifty yet." He looked as if he were a vigorous man, and the way his lips parted in anticipation of speech seemed to reveal enthusiasm as a part of his nature.

Prudence could not take her gaze from him and as his attention was on Andrew Judson he was unaware of her searching eyes. On a day when, for the sake of propriety, all the men present had dressed somberly, this unknown sympathizer had chosen to wear a bright blue stock, and it was knotted with care. Prudence wondered why he had done such a thing; then a sudden delight filled her. She knew exactly why he had done it, and knowing it made her feel an acquaintance that depended not on name or introduction. He did it because he wanted to. It was precisely her reason for doing many things. He was his own master and in all matters where he could best consult with himself he followed his own dictates, regardless of approval or opinion. A girl was sitting beside him, too young to be his wife, and there was a curious resemblance between them.

The man turned suddenly and his eyes met Prudence's gaze. She felt color mounting in her cheeks and reached hastily for her fan.

Mr. Judson's voice thundered on, "—white person coming from another country can be made a citizen by naturalization, but a black one cannot—the law is so—Congress not mistaken when they supposed the spirit of the Constitution gave to white persons alone the right of citizenship. Indians are not citizens—never can be made citizens—why?—answer is obvious—they are persons of color—"

The air was oppressive in the Courtroom and Prudence found it difficult to hold her attention on the speaker. She felt aware of the heat, of the wooden chair she sat on, of the moisture on the palms of her hands. She dared not let her gaze roam again, fearful she might meet the eyes of the man who sat beside Levi Kneeland.

"An American citizen," Mr. Judson was saying. "That proud term means something more than a slave—it means a white man who can enjoy the highest honors of a republic, the privilege of choosing his rulers, and being one, himself."

Prudence sighed, wondering why she had not thought to establish a school for legislators.

By the speed and emphasis with which Mr. Judson spoke and by the way in which he ceased looking into the room but confined his attention solely to the Jury, it was evident that he was approaching a conclusion.

"This is not the case of the town of Canterbury alone against Prudence Crandall—it is the case of the State of Connecticut, and every town, however remote, and every citizen, however unconcerned, has involved in it a deep interest. Let the law be pronounced unconstitutional, by this high tribunal, and a corresponding school for males will be immediately established in some other town—the law is made for the preservation of the State. Public policy demands it. Its resistance is only for the purpose of sowing the seeds of disquiet at the South, and let it not be said that a jury in Windham County commenced the work of dissolving the Union. I leave this case in your hands, trusting that you will return a verdict which shall do honor to yourselves and your country."

Mr. Judson sat down, taking a handkerchief from his pocket to wipe his florid face.

The defense rose. Briefly but brilliantly, Mr. Goddard, Mr. Strong and Mr. Ellsworth spoke in turn, producing facts from history, and opinions of lawyers in the United States and in England on the unconstitutionality of the Black Law. Their appeals were made to reason, and each one exhibited a cool assurance that reason would win the minds of the people.

"This is power," Prudence thought as she listened entranced to the words that were so cogent and convincing, and listening, she wondered how anyone could disagree.

The defense was quick to pick up the admission made by the prosecution that Connecticut could not withhold from citizens the rights they enjoyed in other states.

"Providing they are citizens," Mr. Bulkeley added.

"Which freed Negroes are not," Mr. Welch interposed.

"Why should a man be educated who cannot be a freeman?" Andrew Judson threw out his question.

There was a murmuring among the people on the benches.

"Order!" Judge Eaton commanded.

The counsel for the defense held to their stand based on the Declaration of Independence that Negroes were citizens— "And the citizens of each State shall be entitled to all privileges and immunities of the citizens in several states," Mr. Goddard said, his tone calm with certainty.

When both sides had concluded their arguments, Judge Eaton turned to the Jury. "Gentlemen of the Jury," he said, "as far as the facts are concerned, you alone can determine whether the law has been broken. As to the character of the law, it is the duty of the Court to state an opinion, and the opinion is that the law is constitutional. However, since this is a criminal case, the State gives you the right to decide both the law and the fact."

The jury filed out of the Courtroom. Judge Eaton declared a recess and the room quickened with noise and movement. People began talking together, leaving chairs and benches, going outside to stand under the trees or seek some refreshment. The defense lawyers left the room together, followed by Andrew Judson and his colleagues; but once outside the two groups went in opposite directions. An attendant came with a plate of food for Prudence and a glass of water.

An hour later the Court assembled again and the jury returned from their deliberation.

"You have the verdict?" Judge Eaton asked.

The foreman rose and faced him. "Your honor," he said, "we cannot agree."

The jury was dismissed again and the people in the Courtroom waited, whispering together. Some of them unfolded large, white handkerchiefs and spread them over their faces as if to take a brief rest under shelter. Prudence shifted in her chair. She was beginning to feel extremely tired, weary of words and eager to return to her work, but there was nothing for her to do but pass the time in patience.

The jury returned, only to announce that they could not agree.

"I ask you to try again," Judge Eaton said, "while we await your decision."

Another hour passed while the people in the Courtroom waited for the jury to arrive at their verdict. Slowly the men filed back into their seats and for the third time their foreman faced Judge Eaton.

"Your honor, there is no probability that we will ever agree. Seven of our number are for conviction, five for acquittal."

Judge Eaton looked thoughtfully across the room, avoiding the direct gaze of anyone present. He raised his gavel and let it come down on the desk. "The Jury is excused. I declare the case of Prudence Crandall versus the State of Connecticut to be discharged until a new jury can be assembled. The bonds posted for the prisoner remain in effect until the next term of the County Court in December."

The pensive expression that had rested on Prudence's face brightened visibly when she knew the tedious day had ended and she was to all extents and purposes free. Nothing had been settled, but that nothing was time on her side. Deeply grounded in the principles of her Quaker upbringing, she firmly believed that if one opponent refused to fight, the fight would cease. She sat quietly until the Courtroom had cleared of all but her friends who soon surrounded her.

"You have served the Cause greatly today," Samuel May was first to speak to her, clasping her hands in his.

"The Cause?" she queried, for the words seemed almost meaningless against her fatigue. "What have I done but sit here?"

"All you can do. There is valor in endurance."

George Benson and Charles Burleigh approached her, offering their praise for her conduct and assuring her of the reports they would give the trial in their respective papers. Levi Kneeland took her hand in his. Their eyes met. "You have my sympathy," he said quietly. "No one of us here can do what you are doing for the Cause."

"Always it is the Cause," she murmured. Her lips felt stiff from the long day of silence. "Is there nothing—"

The stranger who had sat beside Levi Kneeland now stood beside him and Mr. Kneeland looked from Prudence to him. "Miss Crandall, allow me to present to you my friend and fellow minister, Reverend Calvin Philleo."

Prudence held out her hand and felt it closed in a firm warm clasp. She raised her eyes and smiled faintly.

"The day must have wearied you, Miss Crandall," Mr. Philleo said in a voice that conveyed a warmth like that of his handclasp.

"Indeed, it has, and I am quite ready to leave this place."

"You must all come to my house for some refreshment." Samuel May looked around the group. "Our women folk have been preparing through the day for our return, but they will wish we had better news." He started from the room.

Calvin Philleo put his arm around a young girl who was now standing close to him, her auburn hair on a level with his broad shoulders. "This is my daughter, Elizabeth, Miss Crandall. Since her mother died two years ago, Elizabeth accompanies me everywhere."

Prudence smiled at Elizabeth and took the girl's hands in hers. "You must be tired, child, from such inactivity. May she not run ahead of us to the parsonage, Mr. Philleo?"

"May I, Papa, please?"

"Why, of course, daughter. I had not thought—"

Before he could finish speaking, Elizabeth had run from the room.

"Restriction is something young limbs cannot bear for long," Prudence said. She rose from her chair, and when Mr. Philleo offered her his arm, took it graciously. "Do you live near here, Mr. Philleo?" she asked as they started from the room, following at a slower pace the brisker movements of the others.

"Once, but now no longer," he answered. "I am a preacher and it has been my way to go wherever opportunity offers as my church grants me that liberty. Now I am on my way to a pastorate in Ithaca, New York."

"So far!" she exclaimed. "Will you be there long?"

"A year, in any case, but I assure you, Miss Crandall," he added, "that my support will ever be with you though I myself should be at a distance."

"With *me*?" Her strained tired face looked up into his. There were many who had rallied to her side, but with them all—Garrison, May, Buffum, Benson, Tappan— it was the Cause of Anti-Slavery that was the real matter, and interest in her seemed dependent on what she could do for the Cause. Here was a man who, completely unknown to her up to a few minutes ago, had come to her support because she was Prudence Crandall.

"Yes, Miss Crandall," he was saying, "why should that surprise you?"

"Only that I hear so much talk of the Cause, as if—" her tone softened with apology, "as if I did not matter."

"A cause is dependent first on individuals. It pleases me to see people for what they are in themselves."

The air that had been so hot and wearying in the Courtroom seemed balmy and sweet once they were outdoors. The streets were almost deserted of people. The trees cast long shadows as the sun approached the horizon. The stillness of a late August afternoon rested on the village. No birds sang and the crickets had not yet commenced their chorus.

Arm in arm they walked toward the Mays' house. Prudence, breathing deeply, felt refreshed, but it was not the balmy air that was doing it so much as the exchange of ideas and viewpoints with a man whose sympathies linked with hers, and whose mind was active, enquiring and immense in its fairness. In all her years, and particularly during the events of the last year that had brought her in touch with so many kindred spirits, Prudence felt that she had met no other person with whom she could share the deep things.

She wished that the distance they had to walk were twice as long; even three times would not be enough for all there was to say. Yet whatever they discussed, with Calvin Philleo the main desire was to see both sides. "One cannot understand without forgiving, Miss Crandall, nor can one forgive without understanding."

On the doorstep he released her arm. "Miss Crandall, as I am in possession of my own conveyance, may I have the signal honor of driving you to Canterbury whenever you desire to leave this gathering?"

The smile she turned on him illuminated her face. "Yes, indeed, Mr. Philleo, and then perhaps the six miles will give us time to discuss these many things in which we have a mutual interest."

The door was opened by Lucretia May. "Prudence, how tired you must be! Samuel says the day was an ordeal."

Prudence tossed her head. Color had returned to her cheeks and her eyes were shining. "Indeed, I am not in the least tired. Mr. Philleo and I walked slowly because we found much to talk about."

"Elizabeth has gone out to play with the children, Mr. Philleo. Your rooms are ready for the night and we are glad that Levi Kneeland will share you with us."

"Thank you, dear Mrs. May, I shall ever be beholden to you."

Samuel May came forward to greet them. "Prudence, you look fresher than you did this morning! I declare, Calvin, she is like a horse that grows bolder with the smell of battle."

"Poor girl, so you must face another trial in December!" Lucretia May exclaimed sympathetically.

"Yes, but the school will go forward until that time," Prudence rejoined.

"The school will go forward," Samuel repeated, "and with it, the great slow-moving mass of public opinion."

A few hours later, sitting in the chaise behind the black gelding who trotted along the level road and slowed to a walk on the hills, Prudence Crandall and Calvin Philleo found there was nothing to talk about. The air of the summer night was warm. The moon was at the full, and the world that lay between

Brooklyn and Canterbury had been turned to silver. Great circular masses of shade lay under the trees; rectangular masses reached from houses and barns. Across the meadows mist was lying. Hummocks and small hills rose out of it like islands; often it seemed as if the road followed the shore of the sea for the stretch into space the mist gave to the land. A whisper of wind in the leaves of trees that arched over the road only made the silence of the night more audible. Coming up the hill into Canterbury, the spire of the Meeting House could be seen, a slender needle threaded with strands of luminous cloud, stitching a pattern on the sky. A hush, a serenity, rested over all created things and there seemed no need to break it with words.

Approaching the center of the village, Calvin Philleo reined the horse to a walk to draw out the time.

"And you will not be at Packerville church with Mr. Kneeland this Sunday?" Prudence asked.

"No, Elizabeth and I leave tomorrow for Ithaca. The new pulpit claims me and there is more work than preaching the Gospel. The church is encumbered with a debt which I shall endeavor to relieve within the year; there is need of a bell in the tower and the establishment of a library."

"You speak as if you expected to accomplish all those matters."

"Indeed, I do."

Prudence watched the wheel of the chaise slowly

revolving. "Will you—" she hesitated, "will you ever return to Connecticut?"

"Yes, I shall return, for it is among these hills and woods that most of my life has been passed. As a boy I was apprenticed to a blacksmith, but I soon fitted myself for the ministry. It was in Suffield that my happiest years were passed; the years in Pawtucket were saddened by the death of my wife."

"It must comfort you to have Elizabeth with you."

"Elizabeth is little more than a child, though she has admirable capacities in woman's work." He sighed, as memory overcame him. "What does comfort me is the remembrance of nearly twenty years of happiness with Elizabeth's mother." His tone changed. "That fine house that exhibits such aristocratic assurance, could that be yours?"

"Yes," Prudence smiled, "that is my home and my school."

He reined the horse to a stop. The house, staunch, square and beautiful in its massive simplicity, wore the moonlight like a fragile shawl. Everything about it was neat and orderly, so much so that the broken pane of glass in one of the front windows was noticeable.

"I grieve to see the evidence of destruction during your absence."

Prudence shook her head. "That stone was hurled through the window one afternoon last week, Mr. Philleo. I do not intend to have the glass repaired until winter winds force me to."

"You have your own reasons, I feel sure, for whatever you do."

"Indeed, I have! The citizens of Canterbury have ever been proud of the dignity and refinement of their town. I would have them be equally proud of their marksmanship." She placed her hand on his knee to restrain him. "Please, Mr. Philleo, do not leave the chaise or come to the door with me. I would have you remain where you are."

"As you wish, Miss Crandall." Then he looked earnestly at her. "May I ask something of you?"

"If it is within my power—" her voice was hesitant.

"From time to time, will you not convey your thoughts to me by means of the post? I cannot hope to return to these parts for at least a year."

"I am no letter writer, Mr. Philleo," she said, her voice betraying her delight. She smiled at him, as much with her eyes as with her lips. "But I will do my best to keep you informed."

"Nor am I a letter writer," he assured her, "though I suppose I have written more than a cart full of sermons. However, imperfect as our abilities are, we must find a way of communication across the intervening distance."

Prudence got out of the chaise. She glanced toward the house to see if any light was burning, but all was dark. She turned back and gazed up at Calvin Philleo. The moon was silvering his hair, softening his face. "Good night, Mr. Philleo, and my thanks are yours."

"Good night, Miss Crandall, and good-by." The whispered words merged into the silence of the night.

Prudence Crandall walked decorously over the path and up the steps as a schoolteacher should. Calvin Philleo spoke to his horse and flicked the reins, sitting straight in the seat as a minister should.

Prudence stood by the door for a moment, part of its shadow. She wanted to hold in her ears the sound of a voice that had spoken to her heart. She opened the door softly and tiptoed up the stairs to her bedroom, but Almira heard her.

"Sister," she whispered, getting up from the bed and running across the room to fling her arms around Prudence. "What has happened? Is all well with the school? Has thee been acquitted?"

"Yes, all is well, indeed," Prudence sighed ecstatically.

"Then the case went in thy favor!" Almira's clasp tightened around Prudence and she looked eagerly into her sister's face. "Oh, I was sure that it would!"

Prudence met Almira's gaze as she tried to recall the events of the day. "There was no verdict, Almira; the case has been bound over until the next County Court. We will continue with our teaching until then."

Almira was puzzled. "Thee seems so happy, Sister. Never have I seen such a look on thy face."

Prudence broke away from Almira's embrace and went to the window. She longed to have one more glance of the chaise and the black gelding as they went over the road to Brooklyn.

“It’s the moonlight, Almira,” she said as she gazed out of the window. “It turns everything to silver. Even the future. Even the way one must walk.”

Tried Again

The dusty heat of late summer hung over the land. Most of the crops had been harvested, many of the pastures had been cropped close, streams were reduced to small trickles; but apples were ripening on the trees, squash and pumpkins gave color to faded fields, the air was sweet with the fragrance of ripening grapes. Prudence Crandall's scholars, now numbering twenty, had returned from brief visits to their homes. Each was well aware that coming to school was like joining a beleagured fortress, but there was not one who did not have faith in her commander.

"My mama says you are the most prayed for woman in the United States," Eliza Gasko announced, "and that anyone near you is bound to get some good."

Prudence accepted the remark. "But I would not have you rely on the efforts of others, Eliza."

The girl, wondering what her teacher meant, looked puzzled.

"Miss Prudence," Maria Robinson came running into the room. "I heard someone on the stage ask the driver where Connecticut was and what do you think he said? He said it was one of the Barbary States!" She laughed. "I wanted to tell him they were on the other side of the world, but my mama told me not to open my mouth when I was on the stage."

"Maria," Prudence asked hastily, "how was it the stage would carry you?"

"My mama got a veil for me to wear. She wore one, too, when she put me on the stage."

"Oh," the eagerness in Prudence's voice subsided.

The child, conscious that she had said something that disturbed her teacher, reached out and touched Prudence's hand. "You didn't mind my coming on the stage, did you, when most of the other girls came by private carrier?"

"No, no, Maria," Prudence replied, "I mind only that you had to wear a veil."

"But it was such a pretty veil, Miss Prudence, the prettiest my mama could find in all the stores in New York!"

The girls, unpacking their trunks, brought out few clothes as the rule of the school forbade many, but they had loaves of bread and boxes of foodstuffs, a baked chicken, a boiled ham, bags of flour and loaf sugar which they gave to Prudence and Almira to help out in the kitchen. Always there appeared some little token of love: a neatly stitched handkerchief, a pair of wristlets for winter wear, a thimble case. Ann Eliza Hammond had fashioned some straw flowers into a nosegay.

"Put it on the mantel by the clock, Ann Eliza," Prudence said, pleased at the mixture of colors in the bouquet. "My sister and I shall see it whenever we look for the time."

The girl went to the mantel and placed her flowers at one side of the clock. There was nothing else on the mantel but a stone the size of a small cabbage. Ann Eliza's supple fingers felt the contour of the stone. It was rough and gray, such a one as might have lain in a field pushed up through successive years of frost, until it broke the surface, and some farmer, gleaning his spring harvest of stones, took it from the field and lodged it in a wall.

Ann Eliza lifted her inquiring fingers from the stone and turned around to face her teacher. "There must be something special about that stone. Could it be a meteor, Miss Prudence? Miss Almira was telling us about them in our astronomy lesson a while back."

"'A while back' is a loose way of speaking, Ann Eliza. Was it in June when you studied about meteorites, or was it only last week? If you think before you speak, you will speak more correctly."

"Yes, Miss Prudence." The girl folded her hands and stood quietly. "It was in July. Could it be a meteorite?"

"No, for a meteorite has streaks of metallic iron in its composition. This is a piece of igneous rock from a nearby field. It was thrown through the front window and landed on the floor of this room."

The girl stared. "But—" she began, "but why do you keep it, Miss Prudence? Why do you keep it *there*?"

"It is a reminder to me, Ann Eliza, of something I wish never to forget. It is also a foundation stone. Such missiles may be used someday in the building of a new school."

"I'd like to take it in my two hands and throw it back at them."

Prudence shook her head. "So long as you or any of the other girls feel that way, Ann Eliza, the stone is in its right place. Until you can look at it without passion, it will remain there."

The days moved on, bringing to Prudence, through the increase in scholars and the support of friends, the evidence of prosperity. Nothing was allowed to interrupt the even tenor of work in the schoolroom. Only when the girls went out for their afternoon walk were they aware of tension in the town, but indignities and annoyances called forth only more fortitude and a loftier spirit. Taking their cue from Prudence, the girls held their heads high and disregarded the inconveniences that beset them.

A few of the townspeople began to show signs of relenting in their attitude, but no attempt was made by the Crandall household to obtain supplies from the local stores, milk from the peddler, or the services of Dr. Harris. When the shallow well in the kitchen went dry in late summer, Pardon Crandall soon brought a barrel of water from his spring, and with it a basket of apples and a gigantic squash that was the pride of his vines.

"Thee is indeed a success," he said to Prudence, "though I am mindful, daughter, that success is capable of many definitions."

"I have room for more scholars, Father, and they will come in time."

"Thee is softer, of late, daughter, and I like thee better. Even with so much running contrary, thee acts as if everything were going thy way."

"Father," Prudence looked around the room to make sure that no one had entered the kitchen, "tell me, Father, when thee met mother, was it love at the first sight?"

Pardon looked at her quizzically, but Prudence turned from his glance and busied her hands with the apples he had brought. He was silent, as memory took him back through the years.

"There was a time, daughter, when I did not believe in love at all, and then—after I met Esther—it seemed there was never a moment in my life when love did not rule. First sight, or forever sight, it seems all the same now. Once there is the sight, nothing dims it."

"Not even distance, Father?"

"Not even death, daughter."

Prudence caught her breath and smiled at her father, feeling a bond with him she had never known before. Then, suddenly aware of color mounting in her cheeks, she murmured that she would send Almira to him and ran from the room.

Pardon watched her go, moving his head slowly up and down. "And who was I to think she would not know happiness?" he said to himself, "though I doubt if it comes easy. Prudence was not born for ease in life."

As the weeks passed and the winds of the changing season tore leaves from the trees, winds of trouble whistled around the school. Scarcely a day went by without a lawyer appearing with a letter of authority from the state, to demand that the scholars give testimony about Miss Crandall and the school. Acting according to their own desire, the scholars from the oldest to the youngest, from the latest arrival to Sarah Harris, stoutly refused to testify. And Prudence was glad. Words wrung from them through repeated questioning could so easily be twisted and turned. Prudence called upon her own lawyers for advice and they maintained that testimony should not be given.

The wrangling went on until the court ruled that

Eliza Gasko must take the stand. She refused, but her refusal only put her in the hands of the sheriff, who escorted her to Brooklyn jail. Eliza, high-headed and serene, felt like an Elisha donning a master's mantle because she was following in her teacher's footsteps. Prudence was distressed, but when Marcia, who had accompanied Eliza to Brooklyn, brought words that Reverend Kneeland had also been put in jail for refusing to give testimony, she knew the publicity that would result from such an indignity could only aid her cause.

When the lawyers approached William Burleigh he gave his testimony willingly, but it provided them with no new arguments. All he would say under oath was that the colored girls he had been teaching in Miss Crandall's school made as good if not better progress than the same number of white girls taken from the same position in life.

The net the prosecution had been employing weakened with Mr. Burleigh's words; it fell apart completely with Mary Benson's. Brought into Court before Andrew Judson, Attorney for the State, she answered freely and fairly every question put to her, but all her answers hung on one statement—that Miss Crandall admitted breaking the law and why should she not break it since it had not been proved to be constitutional. No one denied, said Mary Benson, that the school harbored girls from outside the State, as well as many born within the borders of Connecticut.

She spoke with enthusiasm of her frequent visits to the school and with admiration of the work she had seen accomplished when she attended classes.

Mary Benson's frank attitude served as an impetus. Following her example, Levi Kneeland and Eliza Gasko now announced their willingness to testify. Their remarks were in harmony with Mary Benson's and once given, they were soon released from jail. Everything said had been in Prudence Crandall's favor, but the prosecution had what it wanted and began its work on summarizing the case for the new trial.

Late in September an attempt was made to arrest Almira, but the writ served on her could not be validated and the attempt was a failure. Almira took it in good humor and threw herself with even more energy into helping Prudence prepare for Mr. Tappan's visit in October. The philanthropist had visited the school before, but this was the first time they had been able to prepare a real welcome for him. Others had been invited to mark the occasion, parents, patrons, and friends.

"This will be more than one of our usual Exhibition Days," Prudence said to Almira. "Let us call it a Mental Feast and trust that what we present to our guests will amply feed them."

They sat up late the night before the gala day—Almira taking the last stitches in the white dresses the girls would wear, and Prudence making copies of a ballad she had composed. Before going to bed,

Almira looked from the window wondering what the weather might be like the following day.

"The stars are bright and the wind is sharp. I think, Sister, that the morrow will be fair for our visitors."

"It will be comforting to have the sun shine on our endeavors," Prudence commented. She took from her desk a list of names and glanced at it thoughtfully. "Arnold Buffum, George Benson, Samuel May, Arthur Tappan. I would that Mr. Garrison were to be here, but he has not yet returned from England. I do believe, Sister, that I will ask Levi Kneeland to pronounce a blessing before we commence."

Almira turned from the window. "Oh, Sister, Marcia brought a message from him and I did not give it thee earlier, not wanting to distress thee. He is not well, Sister. He will not be present."

"Not—well?"

Almira shook her head. "I fear the days he spent in Brooklyn jail took from him a toll of strength."

Prudence said nothing for a moment. "Oh, Almira, I am indeed grieved to hear that."

Almira went to her and slipped her arm around her. "He will soon be himself again. By Sunday, when we go to church, he will be in his pulpit, vigorous as always. You will be able then to tell him all about our Mental Feast."

"I could not bear to lose Levi Kneeland," Prudence said, "he is my friend."

"Sister, thee has tired thyself out today or thee

would not take this so to heart. Thee has so many friends, and more all the time."

"I know I have many friends, but there are so few who stand close to one's heart, so very few."

"I am going to bed now, Sister, will thee come too?"

"Soon, Almira."

After Almira left, Prudence turned the lamp out and sat for awhile in the flickering light and diminishing warmth of the fire. An immense loneliness had taken possession of her, and with it despair. It was nothing new, although it was something she did her best to hide from others. Levi Kneeland was her link with Calvin Philleo; their letters passed in his care. Levi had introduced them to each other and though Prudence had said little to Levi, she had the comfort of knowing that he knew of the ripening friendship. The secret world from which she drew such strength was as sacred to Levi as it was to her. She felt that she could endure anything directed against herself, but she did not want him to suffer because of her.

"Not unto him but upon me, O God, if there must be wrath that Thy purpose be served," she prayed, as she sat in the fire lit darkness with an aching lonely heart. But she could not pray for Levi Kneeland without praying as well for the man who stood like a shadow behind him, the man whose auburn hair was streaked with silver and whose voice was like minister and choir in one.

She did not move when she heard the sound for it

had become so familiar—stealthy footsteps, whispering in the shadows, and then the spatter and stench, as the house was pelted with rotten eggs. One, well aimed, came in through the broken glass she had not yet had repaired. By the thud it made it had landed against the lace curtain and broken before the shell fell to the floor. Prudence drew in her breath and sighed, then she went upstairs to bed.

The next morning Marcia called her to the parlor to see what had happened. She had already swept up the fragments of egg shell and washed the floor, but she was distressed about the curtain and wanted to wash it immediately.

"The sun is shining, Miss Prudence, and there's a nice breeze. It would dry before the visitors come."

Prudence's fingers ran over the hardened egg yolk; even washing would not remove the stain from the lace. She shook her head. "No, Marcia, Mr. May will be here any moment, and the stage is due from New York with Mr. Tappan within an hour. We shall let the curtain hang as it is."

When the visitors had all arrived and were seated in the parlor waiting for the Mental Feast which they had been promised, Samuel May commenced it with leading them all in prayer. Then, at a signal from Prudence, who sat in the back row, and prompted by Almira, who stood in the passage with the girls grouped around her, the scholars filed into the room and stood in two lines. Their hands were folded before them, their bodies were relaxed, but it was impossible for them to control their faces. Smiles spread across them, shy and swift at first, then broad and pleased as they gazed out into the room full of people. Half in welcome, half in approval, the audience clapped vigorously. As the sound ceased, Sarah Harris stepped forward.

"Miss Prudence Crandall has asked me to recite for you 'Words on Education' by Mrs. Hannah More." Sarah swallowed and lifted her head, fixing her eyes on a middle distance so nothing would distract her. "'Education is not that which is made up of the shreds and patches of useless arts,'" she began in a measured tone, "'but that which inculcates principles, polishes the taste, regulates temper, cultivates reason, subdues the passions, directs the feelings, habituates to reflection, trains to self-denial, and—'" she paused, reaching into memory for the rest which though firmly implanted had momentarily escaped.

"'And refers—'" a quiet voice from the back of the room prompted.

Sarah's smile was a flash of gratitude as she went on to the end, "'And refers all actions, feelings, sentiments, tastes and passions to the love and fear of God.'"

There was a clapping of hands. Sarah sat down and Emila Willson stepped forward to read a composition of her own. One by one the older girls displayed their ability in reading poems and essays they had written themselves, or in reciting fragments of literature that had been committed to memory. Four of the youngest children stepped forward. Eyes shining, rebellious curls coaxed into order, they stood ready for their part. Happy in the white dresses Almira had made for them with such care, they were proud of the words they had been chosen to recite.

The smallest of the four put one foot behind the other and curtseyed to the audience. "Our words were written by our teacher, Miss Prudence Crandall," she announced in a high clear voice, "especially—" she stumbled over the big words, "especially for this oc-occasion." She moved back in line with her companions. Joining their hands together, the four spoke earnestly and in unison—

"'Four little children here you see,
    In modest dress appear;
Come, listen to our song so sweet,
    And our complaints you'll hear.

'Tis here we come to learn to read,
    And write and cipher too;
But some in this enlightened land
    Declare 'twill never do.

The morals of this favored town,
    Will be corrupted soon,
Therefore they strive with all their might,
    To drive us to our homes.

Sometimes when we have walked the streets
Saluted we have been,
By guns, and drums, and cowbells too,
And horns of polished tin.

With warnings, threats and words severe
They visit us at times,
And gladly would they send us off
To Afric's burning climes.

Our teacher, too, they put in jail,
Fast held by bars and locks!
Did e'er such persecution reign
Since Paul was in the stocks?

But we forgive, forgive the men,
That persecute us so.
May God in mercy save their souls
From everlasting woe!"

There was a great clapping of hands and many of the guests turned around to smile appreciatively at the author. Prudence stood and signaled to the girls to leave the room, but the line remained standing and no one so much as turned toward the door. Almira, alarmed that the girls had forgotten their carefully rehearsed procedure, beckoned from her place in the doorway, endeavoring to catch someone's eye.

Ann Eliza stepped forward and the audience settled into quiet as they realized there was another part to the program. Looking beseechingly at the people and speaking as if the words came from her heart and not from her memory, she informed them that since the by-word of the school was forgiveness, though grievous things had happened on the outside, no one would allow the spirit of retaliation to gain a seat within the school. Daily and hourly their teachers used the utmost care to persuade them not to indulge in angry feelings but to forgive at all times and in every way, so they might be at peace with all men in a true Christian spirit.

Ann Eliza had no difficulty remembering her lines and her words poured from her with eager entreaty. "Let the motto—forgive, forgive—be engraved on every heart, and let this principle of moral excellence be established through the wide earth, till all shall be forgiven, both in this and in that world—" She stepped back into the line and became one with the other nineteen girls, different only in that she was the tallest. They joined hands and twenty voices spoke as one the final lines,

"Where all the just surround the throne,
Both white and sable too,
And there partake the feast prepared
For Gentile and for Jew."

Then the girls turned and walked with dignity from the room.

Once in the passage, relief and delight took over and decorum was forgotten. Some ran down the stairs to help Marcia with the refreshments, some ran up to their rooms, but any noise they made was drowned by the guests talking with each other and with the Crandall sisters.

"Prudence, in future I shall ask you to write my sermons," Samuel May came up to her, beaming.

"But, Samuel, I—"

George Benson, notebook in hand, pushed his way toward her. "Miss Crandall, surely you have a copy of the last recitation? It must appear in *The Liberator,* word for word."

Prudence shook her head. "I knew nothing about Ann Eliza's remarks, nor did my sister. They were the girl's own."

"You mean you did not write them for her?"

Prudence looked honestly into the faces of the men before her. "No, gentlemen. The ballad spoken by the little ones was my own composition, but the sermon was my scholar's."

Arthur Tappan came toward her and grasped her hand in his. "All I can say, Miss Crandall, is that your scholars are a credit to you. It is one thing to imbibe knowledge; it is a far greater thing to become imbued with the spirit of the teacher."

"Oh, sir, I do thank you!" Prudence looked at him

as one of her rare and radiant smiles lit her face.

"Be patient, dear lady, a little while longer and you will see the results of your work. When emancipation is achieved, your school will be found to have played no small part."

"Mr. Tappan, could that be so?"

"Indeed, yes, Miss Crandall. There are evidences around us now that antagonism is breaking down and a more friendly opinion stirring. The result of your next trial will surely be conclusive."

"Sir, your words strengthen my spirit."

"My bank account is behind them. Samuel knows that he can draw upon it indefinitely in your defense."

Before Prudence could thank him again for all he was doing in her behalf, he had merged among the gathered guests.

A week later it seemed that it would take more than financial aid to turn the decision in Prudence's favor. Word was received at the school that Prudence must be ready to appear at the Court on October third, rather than in December. A new prosecution had been secured with Honorable David Daggett, Chief Justice of the Superior Court, appointed to preside. At the news Prudence, usually staunch and able to face anything, felt a sudden thrust of fear. Almira turned pale.

"Judge Daggett!" she exclaimed, and the horror in her tone spoke more than any words.

"If ever a man was hostile to the colored people and the cause of Anti-Slavery, it is Judge Daggett," Prudence said. "I have been told that he is a strenuous advocate of the Black Law."

Almira rallied first. "Our friends will help us, Sister. The trial need not go against thee, though it may be an ordeal."

Prudence walked up and down the room. "Our friends!" she exclaimed. "Where are they? Samuel left yesterday with his family for Boston. He will not return for several weeks. Levi is already burdened with ill health, and Father—no, no, I cannot go to him. My troubles have nearly broken him as it is."

"Sister, Samuel will have heard of this, though it has come so suddenly. He will instruct the lawyers what to do."

Prudence walked to the window, turned and walked to the fireplace. She was about to turn again when her eyes were arrested and she stood still. Slowly she reached up with her fingers and let them close around the stone. Almira watched her, wondering what she was going to do.

"I cannot see why thee gives a common field stone a place on the mantel."

Prudence turned around quickly to face her sister. "It isn't common," she said, then she pressed her right thumb and forefinger tightly together.

"What is it thee wants to remember?" Almira smiled, glancing at Prudence's fingers.

"An idea I want to keep hold of during the trial, something that stone ever reminds me of."

Almira laughed with relief that Prudence could admit a weakness of memory.

"If I cannot trust myself to remember, I shall go to the trial with that stone in my reticule."

"Sister, thee must not do anything so foolish!" Almira cried in alarm. "The guards will think thee is carrying ammunition."

"And so I shall be, for my conscience."

Prudence left the room and started up the stairs, but a moment later she returned to stand in the doorway. "Mark my words, Almira, if the day comes when I cannot forgive the wrongs done to me, I shall give up the school."

Almira's eyes widened. She opened her mouth to speak, then she ran across the room and placed her hand on her sister's arm. "Prudence, does thee know what thee is saying?"

"Yes, Almira, I know, and I know that I always do what I say."

Almira smiled and in relief, laid her head on her sister's shoulder. "I think thee will triumph on October third, even though thee stands alone against the world. I think we shall come to call that day our Day of Emancipation."

On the morning of the trial, Prudence and Marcia drove over to Brooklyn. Marcia held the reins while Prudence got out of the chaise at the Courthouse, then Marcia drove across the road to the shade of some trees where she tied the horse. The trial might last all day, she knew, and she had brought with her some food and her needlework. Miss Prudence was likewise well-supplied, for her reticule was heavily weighted with all she had put into it.

Prudence took her place in the Courtroom, acknowledging with a bow the presence of her three lawyers, and looking toward Judge Daggett who preferred not to meet her gaze. She settled herself comfortably in her chair, feeling stabilized by the weight of her reticule.

One by one the defense took the stage, challenging the prosecution and refuting their arguments. Neither Mr. Ellsworth, Mr. Goddard nor Mr. Strong veered from the position they had taken in August, that the Black Law was unconstitutional. As she watched the faces of the jurors, Prudence thought of a row of trees bowing before the force of the wind, this way, then that way.

When the prosecution maligned her motives and acts, she felt herself stiffening in every muscle, her lips were drawn tight across her teeth, her hands were clenched in her lap. The jurors might be a row of trees, but she was a single oak in a wide plain. Her roots went deep, but even the most stalwart oak could crash in a storm and she wondered how long she could endure the turbulence that swept around her.

She took her eyes from the jury and looked at the people in the Courtroom, seeking for the face that had given her such courage two months ago; but it was not there. She closed her eyes and made an effort to close her ears as she endeavored to reconstruct in her memory the man she longed to see. In a certain way he was there, facing the ordeal with her. But it was not his person she was so aware of as his attitude of mind, the fairness that was determined to see both sides with detachment from the people involved. She had had so many conversations with Calvin Philleo in her mind, as well as those on paper, since their meeting, that she found with only a moderate effort of will and recourse to the gesture she had learned from him, of pressing thumb and forefinger together, that she could listen to him as if he were present.

"If all the books were written about slavery were burned to ashes," she could hear him saying in the voice that sent echoes through a church, "if all the words uttered were dissolved into air, it would not matter. The truth stands. Mankind is one. The walls that divide will dissolve, but not if we add to them in any way."

Passionate words were being directed to the jurors but Prudence gave them little heed, for the remembered tones of another voice that flowed on in her inner ear. "While these things are moving, let us pray for and love one another, as children of the same family, seeking to do the will of our heavenly Father."

Prudence opened her eyes and looked squarely at Judge Daggett as he gave his charge to the jury. "It would be a perversion of terms, and the well-known rule of construction to say that slaves, free blacks or Indians, were citizens within the meaning of that term, as used in the Constitution. God forbid that I should add to the degradation of this race of men; but I am bound, by my duty, to say they are not citizens."

Prudence felt desperately tired, weary of legal words, ill-disguising the emotion behind them.

Two years ago in New Haven, Judge Daggett had distinguished himself by just such methods and caused the dissolution of a college for colored youths. His prejudices were known. Yes, Prudence thought, Andrew Judson had done well to secure him for this trial, if trial it could be called. Judge Daggett concluded his charge to the Jury. The twelve men rose from their seats and shuffled out of the Courtroom for their deliberation. Prudence closed her eyes again. She lifted her reticule on to her lap and with her hands felt the contour of its contents. Reaching inside, she drew out a small bottle of camphor which she uncorked and held to her nose. When she put it away, she let her fingers close around the stone.

There was the sound of feet and the scraping of chairs as the jurors resumed their place, but Prudence had no desire to open her eyes and look into their set faces.

"Your Honor," the foreman rose and addressed

himself to Judge Daggett, "we find the prisoner guilty."

Judge Daggett addressed the Courtroom. "You have heard the verdict. The case of Prudence Crandall versus the State of Connecticut is closed."

Prudence opened her eyes. The Courtroom was a scene of confusion. People were shouting; some were cheering; a few sat silent, stunned by the decision.

Mr. Goddard, leaving his colleagues in earnest talk together, came across the room to the chair where Prudence sat.

"So, it is over," she said, but there was no finality in her words, only acceptance of something that had appeared inevitable from the start.

"No, Miss Crandall," Mr. Goddard shook his head and managed a tired smile, "it is only beginning."

"I have heard those words before, Mr. Goddard."

"And you will hear them again, Miss Crandall, and again, until this case is fairly tried."

"What is your intention now?"

"We shall file a bill of exceptions and make an appeal to the Court of Errors. That will bring your case before the highest tribunal in the State."

"How long will such procedure take?"

"It may be months before a hearing will be granted."

"And I shall continue to live under bond?"

"Yes, Miss Crandall."

She rose, conscious of stiffness in muscles and limbs.

"What will you do now, Miss Crandall? Is there anything my colleagues and I can assist you with?"

"Do?" Weariness slipped from her as she saw before her a measure of action. "I shall go back to teaching school."

Mr. Ellsworth and Mr. Strong came up to her, offering her their sympathy and assurance. The Courtroom had been rapidly clearing of people and now only Prudence Crandall and her counsel remained.

"Your school shall not be broken by legal means while there are legal means to defend it." Mr. Ellsworth spoke with conviction.

"No, the school will not be broken," Prudence agreed, and then smiled tiredly at the three men, "but I wonder if I shall."

"You are made of stern stuff," Mr. Goddard said, eager to encourage what seemed to him to be flagging spirits. "Mr. Garrison says the Cause—with such as you to bulwark it—goes forward mightily."

She shook her head and started toward the door. "I am human, gentlemen, and there are times when I feel acutely aware of the fact."

Mr. Ellsworth opened the door and they went outside. The air and sunshine brought invigoration. Prudence turned to her lawyers. "I bid you good afternoon, gentlemen. You have my thanks for your work in my behalf."

"Miss Crandall," Mr. Strong said earnestly, "I beg

of you not to be disheartened at this setback. As we gain time, your defense grows in strength. In the end we cannot fail."

"I am as sure of that as you are," she replied, then she lifted her head and breathed deeply. "My desire for success is something I share with humanity. Good day," she bowed to them in turn, then walked toward the shelter of trees where Marcia was waiting.

"Take the reins, Marcia, and follow the road to Packerville. I feel that I must speak with Mr. Kneeland before the day comes to its close."

"I'm sorry, Miss Prudence, about the verdict."

"Yes, Marcia, so am I, but it is not final. We shall appear again—and again—" Her voice trailed off as she leaned back against the seat of the chaise.

The Stone on the Mantel

Almira drew the curtains as the January wind skirled around the house.

Prudence looked up from the papers on her desk. "It is just a year ago that the idea of the school first took shape in my mind and see how we are flourishing! Thirty-two girls now; we could not accommodate many more."

"Was there good news in Mr. Garrison's letter?" Almira sat down by the fire with her sewing in her lap.

"Indeed, yes! He sent me a small collection of cuttings from newspapers. Dear William, how pleased he is when some member of the press supports his views! Listen to this, Almira, from the Schenectady *Cabinet*, 'the law which condemns this young lady, conceived in malice and brought forth in hate, is one of the most appalling instances of modern barbarity ever recorded.' "

The tiny sound made by Almira's needle against her thimble could be heard. "It must be a wonderful thing, Sister, to feel that from all over the world there are people supporting thee."

"I would that some were nearer at hand!"

"Then thee would not have so much mail!" Almira looked up from her stitching. "Why, Sister, thee even receives letters at Packerville."

Prudence rustled the papers on her desk, then glanced at the clock on the mantel. "Sister, I do believe our clock is losing time again."

"I had not noticed it. Surely it cannot be more than a minute or two a day."

"Even that is too much. Please to ask Mr. Olney to come and attend to it as soon as he conveniently can."

"Yes, Sister."

The winter days passed, and though the attitude of the townspeople was still unyielding, scarcely a week went by that did not bring either in person or through the mail, something to hearten Prudence in her work. Pardon might continue to caution her against pride but all had to admit a certain truth in what *The Liberator* proclaimed to its readers, that her fame was rising and she stood on a pyramid receiving the plaudits of millions.

Early in February an admirer in Scotland sent her a

cutting from the Glasgow *Chronicle* which told of a piece of silver plate which might be seen at the shop of Mr. Alexander Mitchell, Jeweler, in Argyle Street. The plate, subscribed to by the Ladies Auxiliary of the Glasgow Emancipation Society was to be presented to Prudence Crandall as soon as some one was found who would carry it across the sea. The words engraved on the silver surface spoke eloquently—

To
Miss Crandall
of Canterbury, Connecticut,
This small offering is presented,
With affectionate respect,
By
Female friends in Glasgow;
In testimony of their high admiration
of that ardent benevolence, heroic fortitude, and
unflinching steadfastness,
In the midst of wanton and unequalled persecution,
Which Almighty God has enabled her to display,
In her disinterested and noble endeavors,
Destined to be crowned with honor and triumph,
To introduce into the privileges, and elevate in the scale
Of social and religious life,
A long injured class of
Her beloved Countrywomen.

"Blessed are the merciful: for they shall obtain mercy.

Blessed are ye, when men shall revile you, and persecute you, and shall say all manner of evil against you falsely, for my sake.

Rejoice, and be exceeding glad; for great is your reward in heaven."

Another day there arrived a packet of letters and with them several small tokens for the scholars, sent by the ladies and children of Liverpool, England. The Ladies of Edinburgh sent a Bible and a Concordance, with a *Life of Miss Graham,* together with a collection of pincushions, one for each scholar. A beautiful piece of inlaid wood from sympathizers in Wilbeck was delivered one day. It was soon followed by a work bag carefully stitched with Prudence Crandall's initials, while inside the bag were penwipers and pincushions for the scholars.

It was not until the first Saturday in March that the school was able to obtain the services of Mr. Olney from Norwich to attend to the clock in the parlor, but relatively little time had been lost. Mr. Olney was a free Negro and he felt honored to be summoned to the school on a matter of business. When he left, he would take no payment for his work, no matter what persuasion Prudence offered.

"No, ma'am," he said, "It's little enough any of us

can do for you in return for what you're doing for us. Those young ladies are a right fine lot. I'd as soon study from any one when they get to teaching. Miss Crandall?"

"Yes, Mr. Olney?"

"I don't want any of your clocks to lose or gain, but happen they do, I'd be mighty pleased if you'd call on me again."

"Thank you, Mr. Olney. The success of this school is due largely to people like yourself who see the good we are accomplishing and who wish us well."

The next day there was no question in any one's mind as to when all should be ready to leave for church; the parlor clock was right with the town clock and both were right with Pardon Crandall when he arrived at the door, driving one farm wagon, with Reuben following in another. Though early in the year, the world stood on the edge of spring. The river, released from ice, was flowing swiftly. Willows along its banks were greening. Alders and osiers were hung with catkins and the ground at their base was strewn with down. Oxen stood in the fields, enjoying the warmth of the sun and the freedom from work. Sometimes, passing a barn whose doors were open to let in the new warmth, a setting hen could be glimpsed, winking and dozing on a shrunken haymow.

Such peace and promise filled the world that Prudence protested when Levi Kneeland told her after church that he would soon preach no more sermons. The lines of suffering in his face served to underscore his words.

"I knew you were not well," Prudence said. "I had not realized, dear friend . . ." She could not finish, but turned her head away from him and let her eyes follow Almira as she went down the road with the girls, in search of marsh marigolds.

"My sands are running short, too swiftly, I fear, to fulfill one last function—a wedding of two friends."

"Oh," Prudence brightened, "could not the time be advanced for the occasion? A bride with your blessing would be happy indeed."

"Unfortunately, dear Prudence, the bridegroom cannot reach these parts until early August. Six months for one has become for me a lifetime."

"I do not understand. Surely—"

"Duty keeps the bridegroom at a distance. He is a minister and his year is not at an end until the last Sunday in July."

The sound of a quickly indrawn breath came from Prudence.

"However," Levi Kneeland went on, "he has informed his church that because he faces the necessity of being absent a considerable part of the time it would be inexpedient to engage him again."

"Will he," Prudence spoke eagerly, "seek a pulpit in Connecticut?"

"Yes, and he will have no trouble finding one. He is a powerful preacher, possessed of a vivid imagination and remarkable descriptive powers, which he uses to advantage. He is a most energetic man, and so fair, always so fair."

"Has he—" Prudence paused, finding speech had begun to fail her, "has he a noble way of speaking?"

"Indeed, yes! His voice is known for its clearness and sweetness, and his ears so true that it seldom errs in pitch. His power over an audience is unequaled."

"Levi, I—I—"

"Prudence, what is it? Are you not well?"

She put her hands to her face and spoke through them. "I am quite well, but I feel that I must sit down."

Together they walked toward a bench under a tree and sat down. Prudence took her hands from her face and tilted her head up; the sun could not feel warmer than her cheeks just then.

"Prudence, the minister of whom I have been speaking hopes that I may link him in marriage with the one he loves, but I fear that will not be for me to do." Levi Kneeland lowered his voice. "If I cannot bless his wedding, perhaps he can conduct my funeral."

Prudence turned to him beseechingly. "Levi, I cannot bear it. The joy. The pain. They are both so sharp."

"I have been asked to convey to my friend your sentiments," Levi said, trying to mask his delight with sober words. "He cannot return to Canterbury until August, but when he does, he hopes that you will become his wife."

Prudence put her hands up to her face again. She

nodded her head slowly, though she spoke no accompanying words. A few moments later she reached out her hand, wet as it was from the tears she had tried to contain, and laid it on Levi's. She could not look into his eyes, so she kept her gaze on his hand. A strong hand still, though it rested on heaven's gate.

"Even we cannot hold you, can we, Levi, beyond your time?"

He shook his head.

"I have not enough friends to be able to part willingly with you."

"You have many friends, Prudence, and you will have more," Levi said quietly, "and you will win, though it may be in God's time."

She turned and looked at him, her eyes more blue than gray and very bright. "Levi, the trial is set for July twenty-third. I trust there will be a decision before Calvin comes."

"I think you cannot tarry much longer with events of the past, Prudence. It is for you to dedicate yourself to the future."

Prudence's heart had been light with love and hope, but when she went to bed that night it was heavy with foreboding. The air was cool and damp. The frogs singing in the marshes and sounding like sharp-toned sleigh bells kept her awake. When she finally fell asleep it was to dream that she had fainted and Almira was endeavoring to rouse her by passing a burned feather under her nose. She tossed restlessly and drew the sheet over her head, unwilling to awake to a world that held such anguish as the parting of friends. Sleep, fitful and dream ridden, was far better. Suddenly she sat up-right in her bed. It was no dream she was experiencing. The smell of fire was all around her, though there was no flame to be seen in the darkness and no smoke to choke her.

"Almira!" she cried, as she fumbled to light the candle by her bed.

Wide-eyed, Almira sat up, tucking her hair under her nightcap.

"See to the girls, Almira, while I see to the fire!"

Almira threw a blanket around her shoulders and ran to do her sister's bidding.

Prudence, with Marcia who had been hastily summoned, searched the house from the cellar to the attic, room by room, opening cupboards, even pulling out drawers, but though the smell of burning persisted, they could not trace its origin. It was not until daylight came that Prudence, walking around the outside of the house, saw flames suddenly burst out from one of the sills.

"Water!" she cried, as she ran to the well to haul up a bucket of water that though fouled for drinking, could still quench fire.

Marcia came with another bucket, and the girls ran from the house with water in jugs and basins. The flames were soon doused and when the embers had cooled Prudence reached her hands under the sill to feel if any warmth still lingered. Among the charred and sodden wood was a mass of combustibles still unburned. She drew them out—paper, shavings and small dry sticks that had been carefully tucked into a hollowed out place. Burning like a slow match, hours had gone by before the decayed wood of the still had been ignited.

"For months past I have tried to get a carpenter to replace that sill, but none would work for me!" Prudence exclaimed.

An hour later when Prudence and Almira sat with the girls at breakfast, Prudence gave thanks not for the food on their plates, but for a rotten sill which had kept the house from burning while they slept.

The fire might have been merely another inconvenience and as such disregarded had not a delegation of the Civil Authority called on Prudence Crandall two evenings later.

"We are agitated in the extreme, Miss Crandall, to know that your house and the entire town of Canterbury so nearly escaped being reduced to ashes," their spokesman announced.

"It gives me a degree of comfort to receive your apology," Prudence replied.

"That is not the purpose of our visit, Miss Crandall. We are here to tell you that a writ has been served on the culprit and a trial has been set in Brooklyn, the last week in March. Witnesses are required. Every member of your school is herewith served a writ and must attend the trial."

Prudence bowed slightly and made no reply.

"Your act endangered our town, Miss Crandall."

"*My* act?"

"It is well known that you are tired of your school and would like to be rid of it, but it was madness for you to attempt to burn it down."

"Gentlemen, you speak in riddles."

"Of course, you did not do it yourself. Your recklessness would hardly go that far, and your accomplice was not skilled enough in arson to succeed, but he has been arrested and is awaiting trial in Brooklyn jail."

Prudence looked from one to another of the men confronting her. Her eyes were hard and cold; her words were forced between the set line of her lips. "I ask that you explain yourselves."

"You feign ignorance! The whole town knows now, as well as you did two days ago, that the fire was set by the man last seen working in your house, a certain Mr. Olney from Norwich."

"Mr. Olney!" Prudence gasped.

"That is the name of the man awaiting trial for the deed you made him do."

Prudence reached out to put her hand on a chair, momentarily weakened by the indignation that possessed her. "Gentlemen," she said, "that fire was started from the outside."

"Tell that to Judge Adams at the trial," one of the men replied.

"Very well, I shall." Prudence felt herself rallying. "I shall have all the witnesses necessary to speak for me and to clear Mr. Olney of this monstrous charge."

A matter of minutes after the Civil Authority left, a well-known knocking sounded at the door and Marcia ran joyously to answer it.

"When I heard of the latest outrage, dear Prudence, I left my sermon in the writing and rode with all haste to comfort you."

"Thank you, Samuel. Forgive me if I sit down. I have had a moment of weakness and am only just recovering. Marcia, some tea, and tell Miss Almira to join us presently."

"Yes, Miss Prudence."

Prudence faced her friend eagerly, as if she could not gain his counsel too soon. "Samuel, we have suffered indignities and inconveniences, but this is danger. If our enemies are still so malignant, is it right for me to expose the lives of my scholars to their devices?"

"You cannot abandon the school now, Prudence."

"It is not my desire to do so, but if the girls' lives are at stake—"

"I beg of you," he interrupted, "hold on a little longer. The ferocity of this latest attempt will be blazoned forth in the press, not only in *The Liberator* and *Unionist,* but in the other papers that are daring to lift their voices. People will see what the evil is we are combating, and the principle . . ."

"I wonder, Samuel, if there is a principle at stake any longer—" she smiled slightly as she felt herself regaining her customary calm—"or if it is not sheer malice that has taken over the minds of the persecutors."

Steps could be heard in the passage. Almira entered, smiling with friendly welcome. Marcia followed with the tea tray.

Samuel looked at Prudence entreatingly. "Will you not hold on a little longer?"

"Why do you ask, Samuel? You know that I will."

Prudence felt buoyed with new hope when the trial was over in Brooklyn, for it had been something of a festive occasion, with all the girls staying at the Bensons' big house, Friendship Valley, where Mr. Garrison was also a visitor, and herself and Almira enjoying the Mays' warm hospitality. Mr. Olney was soon acquitted. The evidence brought by townspeople in Canterbury was trifling weighed against the evidence produced by her friends and the scholars, all of whom had aided in putting out the fire. Mr. Olney himself was so understanding in his attitude that the whole affair only served to strengthen Prudence. She thought of it as a happy augury for the more impressive trial looming in July.

Greatly encouraged, she went to Boston early in April accompanied by Marcia and was entertained enthusiastically by members of the Anti-Slavery

Society, at formal banquets and in their homes. She even consented, at Mr. Garrison's request, to sit to Mr. Francis Alexander, for her portrait.

Returning to Canterbury with a steel engraving of the portrait, she showed it to her father. "They are being printed in hundreds, Father, and will be sold throughout the nation for the Anti-Slavery Cause."

Pardon looked at it and then at his daughter. "Thee has never gone far from thy place of birth, Prudence, and yet influence streams from thee." His smile enfolded her as his arms had when she was a child.

"Does thee like the picture, Father?" Prudence asked, eager for his word of approval.

He looked at it more closely, then at her again. "The sternness thee can command, daughter, is in it, and the tranquillity thee has achieved; but I doubt if the greatest artist in the land could convey the courage thee has used long and well."

She had need of all her courage and faith for the trial took place in Brooklyn, on July twenty-third, before the Supreme Court of Errors. Again her counsel argued eloquently against the constitutionality of the law; again the prosecution argued stubbornly that the law was consistent with the republic. Through it all Judge Daggett held to his opinion that Negroes were not citizens, though more than one of the judges present inclined to the feeling that he was wrong in his charge. The Court reserved its decision, and a week later issued a statement saying that because of defects in the information prepared by the State's Attorney it was unnecessary for the court to come to any decision.

When Samuel May brought Prudence the news she looked at him helplessly.

"If you can bear, Prudence, to cast your glance far ahead in time you may see, as I do, that this is all to the good."

"I fear, Samuel, that these repeated trials have shortened my vision."

"Feeling between the Abolitionists and those who still advocate Slavery has been running high, and the legal status of the Negro has become a delicate question. The court was afraid to hand down a decision. That was why they quashed the case on purely technical grounds."

"The law has been able neither to save me nor convict me," Prudence commented. "I wonder what effect this will have on the townspeople of Canterbury when they face the fact that their recourse to law has been indefinitely postponed."

Samuel May was silent. When he spoke, the words came almost against his will. "I hope they will not take the law into their own hands."

"I do more than hope, Samuel; I pray."

"I would feel better, Prudence, if during the weeks to come you had a man in the house."

She glanced toward a calendar on her desk. There was only one day left in July. The turning of the page might signify more than the passing of time. She laughed. "Samuel, this household of women has proved able to withstand the attacks of the men of the town. I think we shall be able to hold out a little longer."

There was a knocking at the door, light and tentative at first, then strong and certain.

Marcia came running up the stairs. "Are you expecting anyone, Miss Prudence?"

"No, Marcia, but please to open the door. It is only friends who knock. The townspeople have found entrance in other ways, but surely—" She stopped speaking as the sound of a deeply remembered voice could be heard at the door.

Almira, entering the room from the passage, was alarmed by her sister's pallor and ran hastily across the room to stand beside her.

"I am quite all right, Sister, but if thee can give me a hand I will take it gladly."

Almira held Prudence's hand that was cold and trembling, while Prudence rose and stood unsteadily by her chair.

A tall man, his broad shoulders a little stooped, his cape still showing the dust of travel, stood in the entrance to the room.

"It's a Mr. Philleo come to see you, Miss Prudence," Marcia announced, holding the visitor's hat as if she thought it might fly from her hands.

"Oh!" Prudence gasped, taking a step forward. "Oh, Calvin, I had not thought you would be here quite so soon, I—" She held out her hands to him. The smile that lit her face was eloquent welcome.

Calvin Philleo strode across the room, oblivious to Almira and Samuel May. Holding out his hands, he took both those that Prudence held out to him in his firm clasp. They stood looking into each other's eyes.

"Where—where is Elizabeth?" Prudence asked.

"She is visiting with an aunt for a few weeks," Calvin answered.

Almira's lips trembled with words she could not utter, for in the long look that passed between Prudence and the stranger she saw reason for much that had puzzled her during the year. She had known that Prudence had a secret; now she knew what it was and she was glad.

Almira tapped Samuel May on the shoulder. "Let us join the girls in the schoolroom for a little while." At the doorway she whispered to Marcia, "Please to put the kettle over, Marcia, we shall all want tea, perhaps in half an hour. Would you say that would be ample, Mr. May?"

"Yes, indeed," he smiled. "Half an hour is long enough to settle even the most momentous question."

"It takes half an hour for the kettle to come to a boil," Marcia giggled as she ran down the stairs to the kitchen.

That night the sisters stood by the window watching the two men ride off on their horses, disappearing down the road to Brooklyn.

"What will thee wear for a wedding dress, Sister? Thee must have something with a bit of finery. Such a day comes only once in a lifetime. There is no one in town who will sell us anything and it would take time to go to the shops in Boston or Providence."

Prudence stepped back from the window. Distance had taken away what her eyes had been watching, but darkness had not yet dimmed the room. She looked around her. Her eyes were sparkling and she smiled gaily like a child. Drawing a chair to the window, she stood on it and reached up to detach the lace curtain from the rod that held it, then, stepping down to the floor, she draped the curtain around her shoulders. "Here is my wedding dress, Sister."

"Prudence, it is stained! There are yellow marks on it."

"Let them remain. They speak for me."

For some reason unknown to the scholars in Miss Crandall's school, August twelfth had been declared a holiday. Prudence and Almira had driven off in the chaise to some destination they had not seen fit to tell the girls, but the girls knew it was not to a trial, for never had they seen their teachers look so happy and Miss Prudence was wearing a lace dress and carrying her Bible. During the day, William Burleigh read to the scholars instead of hearing their lessons, and his sister came to help them with their sewing.

Marcia was busy in the kitchen preparing for a

feast, to which all had been invited. Her stove was covered with cooking pots, bubbling and simmering. The thump of her rolling pin and the din of her pestle pounding spices and herbs resounded through the house. By afternoon, table and counters were covered with loaves and pies, cold meats, bowls of custards, and the delicacies that were her delight. She had even found time between rounds of cooking to go to the fields for wild flowers to dress the house.

By six o'clock, when the sun was beginning to slant toward the west and a cooling breeze crossed the heat of the day, all was in readiness, though for what, was anyone's guess. The girls had been sent to their rooms to put on their best clothes and soon after that two chaises and a familiar farm cart arrived at the carriage step. Out of the first chaise stepped Prudence and a tall gentleman, deferentially holding her shawl; out of the second stepped Samuel May and the Reverend George Tillotson; in the farm cart Almira sat beside her father, both in their Sunday best.

"Do you see what I see?" one girl said to another as they peered from an upper window.

"Oh, oh, what a handsome man is walking with Miss Prudence!"

Then there was an excited whispering. The room sounded as if bees were swarming in it.

"I'm so happy for Miss Prudence," an older girl sighed.

"I'm so happy I'm going to cry," one of the youngest said.

The girls ran down the stairs and formed themselves into two lines in the passage. When the door opened they wanted to sing or shout their welcome, but not one of the thirty-two could do anything but smile.

Prudence stood in the doorway with Calvin beside her. She looked down one line of girls and up the other, meeting every pair of eyes with a glance, while her smile included them all. "Girls," she said at last, and her voice quivered with the joy she was feeling, "this is my husband, the Reverend Calvin Philleo."

Late that night, after quietness had taken over the world, Prudence lay wakeful, going over and over in her mind the words of the marriage service, with all their wonder and all their meaning.

"Do you, Calvin, take this woman to be your wife, and do you promise to love, honor, cherish and maintain her as long as God gives you life, health, and ability so to do?"

"I do, sir," Calvin's voice had answered with the power that launched sermons into the minds of his congregations.

"And do you, Prudence, take this man to be your husband, and do you promise to love, honor, cherish and obey him, till death do you part?"

"I do," she had said, hoping the trembling within her would not carry to her voice.

Only one shadow fell across the day and that was Levi Kneeland's absence; but it was he who had brought them together and each one knew that in their united life they would be rearing something of a monument to him.

One day passed then another, and it seemed as if peace had come to Canterbury. There was a festive air in the house and even Prudence could not exact the full due of concentrated work from the girls, when she felt so happy. One week passed, then another, and the girls began to enjoy the pleasure of afternoon walks without incidents.

"Can the presence of a man in the house make this difference?" Prudence asked Calvin one night, before they went upstairs to bed. She leaned toward the calendar on her desk and drew a line through the date, September 9.

"The day is not over yet," he reminded her.

"But the school day is!" she flashed a smile at him, "and this is my school calendar." She picked up her candle and waited while he lit the wick. "I must make my rounds through the girls' rooms to see that they are asleep. In a few moments I will join you in our room."

He watched her go, then walked across the room to stand by the window. It was late, but there were lights in Andrew Judson's house across the road and the sound of voices drifted through the night.

Compared to them, the school seemed singularly quiet and peaceful. Calvin Philleo dimmed the lamp and went upstairs.

Silence came down over the village as one by one all lights went out. The church bell tolled the hours but few heard them, and no one saw the shadows coming from some of the houses and converging on the Crandall school. Stealthily they came, through gates and across the road, gradually surrounding the square white house which stood stalwart under the stars. With clubs in their hands and iron bars raised, they waited until the last stroke of twelve sounded from the church tower. Midnight was their signal to advance.

A moment later and the peace of the night was shattered by the crash of breaking glass, the grinding of wood, as window sashes were torn away and clapboards were wrenched from their ancient hold. Screams filled the air as frightened girls cried for help in high shrill voices. Heads appeared at the window, but as they did the shadows of men with clubs and bars disappeared into the deeper shadow of the night. The roads were empty, the houses dark, and all was quiet in Canterbury except for the confusion in the Crandall school.

Prudence dressed quickly and with Almira hurried to the girls' rooms while Calvin hastened down the stairs to the scene of destruction. Candles were lit. Marcia ran to the parlor and was told by Calvin to drive to Brooklyn as soon as it was daylight and bring Samuel May back with all speed. Nothing Prudence or Almira said or did could restore the girls' confidence. Too stunned to speak, they clung to each other weeping; or reached out trembling hands to their teachers. In drawn faces and bewildered eyes was the question: What would happen to them now?

Gradually their fright lessened and as they became more calm, Prudence felt she could leave them with Almira. She went down the stairs to join her husband. Calvin was in the parlor, sweeping the broken glass into piles.

"I fear the rooms are untenable," he said. "Prudence, you have been able to do without many things but you cannot do without windows to keep out the weather. Ninety panes have gone in all. It will take time to replace them and money, but so long as ill will reigns they are not safe."

"Oh, Calvin, Calvin," she moaned, as her eyes looked at the gaping windows. She shivered in the night air that filled the room.

He went toward her and put his arms around her. "You are tired, dear Prudence, and unstrung. Sit down while I get a cloak to put around you. The room now is as cold as the out of doors."

In the candlelight her face looked white and her lips had drawn tightly together. "I have always hated evil," she said, as the slowly surging fury within her muffled her words, "but now it is the doers of evil I hate as well."

He put his hand through her arm and led her to the sofa. "You are my wife, Prudence, as well as the head of this school. I ask that you sit down and listen to what I have to say."

She stared at him. Amazement quenched the fire in her eyes. "Yes, Calvin," she said, and sat down.

"Prudence, men may destroy your school but they cannot destroy you unless you learn to hate them." His voice was low and he compelled her gaze. "You must stop before that happens."

The shadows cast by the candle in the gusty air were the only movement in the room.

"You mean I must stop teaching?"

He shook his head. "As well to ask you to stop breathing! You must stop teaching here."

"No."

"Prudence, I ask that you abandon the school."

"Calvin, that I will not do!" Her eyes blazed again as she looked at him. "I shall show them yet that we can win."

He held her hands in his, chafing them gently to bring some warmth into them.

Prudence dared not look into his eyes so she turned her head away from him and stared into the room. The darkness of the night was yielding to dawn and the gray light that now began to fill the room showed even more clearly than the restless gleam of the candle the destruction that had been made. Prudence glanced toward the mantel to see the time. Her eyes confronted the stone and her whole being froze in immobility.

A minute might have passed, or an hour, but to Prudence Crandall Philleo it was the better part of a lifetime. She drew her hands away from Calvin's and put them to her head, crying out as if she had been struck.

Her throat had tightened so that she found it difficult to speak. "Will you—always—oppose me, Calvin?"

He took her hands in his again to comfort her. "Call it opposition, if you like," he said quietly. "Love has many names."

"Once I thought it was conscience made one choose what is difficult," she lifted her face to his and smiled bleakly, "now I know it is love. But, Calvin, I had so hoped to win!"

"Can you not see, dear wife, that you may have won?"

She stared at him. His words were meaningless at first, but they gained sense slowly in her mind, and then grew in import. Sitting there in the chill and the changing light she let herself go back over the months of siege in the school, the months of acclaim from the world; but the end had come, not because Calvin had asked her to close the school, not because the stone on the mantel had struck her as if it had been skillfully aimed. No, it was because she herself knew that it was time to give way.

"I suppose there are some seeds for whom germination is long and difficult," she said.

"And there are some whose germination reaches beyond one lifetime," he replied.

There was silence between them, though each one was aware of the other's thoughts. The candle burned down in its socket. Daylight filled the room. Prudence began to nod her head slowly.

"I shall close the school," she said. "It is the only forward step we can take." Her voice was calm, her eyes were steady, though the hard-won position could not be held for long. She buried her head in her hands. "But, oh Calvin," she cried between sobs, "I cannot face the girls just yet—I cannot tell them, after all we have been through—together."

"Nor need you, Prudence, for a little while. When Samuel comes he will talk with them."

Soon after Samuel May arrived the girls were assembled in an upper room and he spoke to them, telling them in words he found hard to utter, that the school was to be closed. "I am ashamed of Canterbury, I am ashamed of Connecticut," he said, "ashamed of my country, ashamed of my color."

The girls looked up at him with faces that might have been cast in bronze. There was nothing any one of them could say in reply.

Two days later the house was empty. The girls had

returned to their homes. Almira had gone to live with her father. Marcia, now free to marry Charles Harris, went to stay with his family. Prudence walked out of the door for the last time and Calvin, closing it behind him, stopped to nail a printed paper on its wooden panels.

FOR SALE

The house in Canterbury, occupied by the late Prudence Crandall, now the wife of the subscriber. The impunity with which repeated assaults have been made upon these premises has awakened the apprehension that the lives of those connected with the school, are insecure. I have therefore thought it proper, and do hereby advertise the house and appurtenances thereof for sale.

For other particulars inquire of the subscriber, or of
Pardon Crandall of Canterbury, or
Samuel J. May of Brooklyn

CALVIN PHILLEO

Canterbury, September 11

Calvin drove the last nail forcefully, then he put the hammer in his pocket, took Prudence's arm and they went down the walk together. He helped her into the chaise and got in beside her. Then he took up the reins and spoke to the horse.

"And we, Calvin, what shall we do now?"

"We can begin again, Prudence, some place else."

EPILOGUE

Elk Falls, Kansas 1886

She was thin and spare, but she bore her years easily. Time had only lightly stooped her shoulders and furrowed her forehead; blue eyes under heavy brows were still bright, and short, sandy, gray hair framed a long face that was still eager. Sitting on a bench outside the pioneer box-house that was her home, she turned the pages of a worn composition book, reading entries that caught her glance. An apple on the bench beside her reflected the low light of the sun. A pencil lay on her lap, its point newly sharpened for the entry she intended making in her Journal, but there was no hurry. Slowly she leafed through the record of the past.

1838, Troy Grove, Illinois . . . Calvin and I are settled now on the land that Father purchased for us. Preaching and teaching suit us well. . . A letter from Almira says Reuben is dead. His health suffered two years ago when he was jailed in Washington, D.C. for distributing copies of *The Liberator* and other so-called "seditious" papers. His time in prison was far longer than mine—six months before trial and acquittal. . . . Almira says Andrew Judson was defeated in the election for congress and that the Connecticut Legislature has voted to repeal the Black Law. Reuben, Reuben, can thee see this first turning of the tide?

1845 The Philleo Academy is flourishing. These young Negroes, many of them so recently slaves, have much natural intelligence but great ignorance of letters. Calvin is not well. I am glad that I am strong, for I know of no way to keep green and growing all that Father lived for and Reuben died for than to teach. Arthur Tappan sends us generous aid. Mr. Garrison is pleased that we feel as he does about woman's rights, political as well as educational.

1850 . . . Samuel writes from Syracuse that he is a station-keeper on the Underground Railway. The slave has many friends and

Samuel says that thousands have already been conducted to freedom. The tide is rising—

1852 Arnold Buffum sends me a book in which he has written, "What Prudence Crandall was to the opening days of the Anti-Slavery Cause, Harriet Beecher Stowe is to the closing." The book is called *Uncle Tom's Cabin.*

1854 . . . a covered wagon train went by our door. The leader stopped for water and I called my boys and girls to meet the people. They are New England men and women, some from Connecticut, and they are on their way to settle in Kansas and help bring the Territory into the Union as a Free State. They know what freedom means and they are daring everything to—

1856 What does it mean, this raid of John Brown's at Pottowatomie? Calvin says immediate news is often shattering but that to read history is to see mankind mounting a ladder, rung by rung. . . . My youngest brother, Hezikiah, has moved with his family to Illinois.

1857 The Dred Scott Decision fills us with sorrow. It is not the slave alone who is bound by chains. What shackles hold the lawmakers of our highest Court! But I refuse to be downcast. Neighbors come to the door in despair, but I tell them this decision is not a defeat. Calvin says I will wear myself out with words, but I feel as I did in the Canterbury days. . . . Seven letters this morning; six of them heavy with fear and foreboding, but the seventh, from Almira, says: "Sister, thee and I know what it means to stand firm against discouragement. And our numbers are growing." Staunch heart and true, how glad I am that the sun of happiness smiles on her days!

1859 . . . raid at Harper's Ferry . . . John Brown captured . . . executed . . . many are saying the Cause is lost, but I tell them—

1861 Journeyed to Springfield to see him take his leave. Never shall I forget that face of tenderness and sorrow, the shoulders bent under the shawl and the grave responsibility he carries. Can he hold this splitting Nation together with those large hands of his? People are wondering, but I was near enough to see his eyes and I—

Fort Sumter has been fired on. Is this the answer to Mr. Lincoln when he says the Government cannot endure half slave and half free? Calvin says the North lacks skill and training, but I say—

January 1, 1863 Defeat has marked the months, underscored the years, and through the gloom the ideal for which we have been striving has grown dim, but Mr. Lincoln has issued his Emancipation Proclamation. Bells peal from every church tower, every school. From this day on, the tide gains force. Now, at last, Negroes will be treated as human beings. I hear God's voice in the pealing of the bells, speaking to us who have labored long to carry on with the work of civilization. Thank God, I am still strong. There will be need for educators. . . . Mr. Garrison writes of addressing some three hundred plantation slaves and asking them to give three cheers for freedom. They were silent, not knowing how to cheer.

April 14, 1865 In a great cause, I have never thought the price of death too high, until now. Where is the unity of heart, mind and hand that belonged to Mr. Lincoln? Each one of us must bear some of the burden that bowed his shoulders. The war may be over, but—

1866 Almira writes that Connecticut has put Negro Suffrage to the vote. She says press and people declared themselves strongly in favor of equal political rights. Windham, with its fifteen towns all capable of independent action, was the banner county leading the State. Suffrage won by a majority of thousands. . . . Samuel writes, reminding me that though I did not succeed in teaching many colored girls I succeeded in educating the people of Windham County. . . . Letters come from my old pupils. Many are going South to help plant the common schools so needed . . . New England is sending an heroic army of teachers, backing them with generous grants. They must do the work I would do. We have had to close the Academy. Calvin is ill and his care requires my time. . . . We move to Mendota, where living will cost less. . . . Eliza Gasko writes of the difficulties . . . Some of the hands released from the cotton fields have never held a book. She must teach grown men the alphabet. General Howard of Vermont is in charge of the Freedmen's Bureau and is doing a great work. Already some thousands of schools have been established.

1867—and this year marks the founding of Howard University in Washington, D.C. for the education of Negro youth. The doubts about the future which once troubled me are now rapidly passing away.

1871 My fingers are laggard for my heart is numb. Samuel has gone. Years and distance have rolled between us, yet always he was there. But I feel him here. I do not ask how that can be, I only know that it is so. Mr. Garrison spoke at his funeral, calling him "a brother beloved incomparably beyond all blood-relationship." . . . went to hear the Jubilee Singers, a group of young men and women from Fisk University. Were these the ones who knew not how to cheer? They sang their spirituals, rising from bondage and sorrow through freedom to responsibility. I quite forget that I am an old lady with no voice better than a hen's cackle when they sang Julia Howe's Battle Hymn. I found myself singing too! Yes, His truth is, indeed, marching on.

1872 A letter has come from a Mr. Andrew White, a friend of Samuel's and president of the Cornell University "wherein any person can find instruction in any study." It is located in Ithaca, New York. Samuel had my portrait in his possession and has left it to Mr. White who tells me it will hang in the University Library. So, I shall look on students again, young men and women, dark-skinned and light! Perhaps I shall have something to say to them. Calvin is glad I am to see Ithaca, though from a frame. He says it is a beautiful—

January 5, 1874, Cordova, Illinois. This day I said goodbye to Calvin. My pen must dip itself in tears to write . . . first test of the marriage vow . . . soon after our wedding when he asked me to give up the school . . . hard then, but the broad wings on which I could rise. It was Calvin who—The years go on and for those of us who live there is work to do. I spend myself now on woman suffrage, temperance, and the formation of an International Arbitration League, and in the only way I know. I turn to children again. I never had any of my own to love, but I love every human being and I want to do what I can for their good.

1878 Hezikiah is farming in Kansas . . . offers me a few acres near him so I am a farm woman again with a barn well-stocked and a small house filled with books. My niece, Clarisa, has come to live with me and Charles Williams whom I have adopted as a son. Life is bare and there is little to go on, but the land and the animals keep us fed. I have friends nearby and my health is good. There are children. Every day they come to the house. We talk about things together and so we learn from each other.

May 24, 1879 Mr. Garrison has gone to join those who have preceded him and with whom he labored. What gallant witness he bore to the brotherhood of man!

1881 . . . and one of my old pupils writes that in the far South a Negro, once a slave, Booker T. Washington, has founded a seat of learning, Tuskegee Institute. . . . so from many sides comes the news, yet none of these changes have happened overnight. People have been working toward them for years and now the results are multiplying. Calvin said something to me once about seeds and their germination. I know why it was not failure in Canterbury when all around me was the evidence of defeat: *I was not alone*. . . . This Nation has acknowledged the wrong it was doing and is making one creative effort after another to right that wrong . . . Negro education . . . Negro suffrage. . . . Once I thought forgiveness was great, now I see repentance to be even greater for it is life-giving. These United States are strong because they have the capacity to see and correct mistakes, to change and grow. The sentiments of the Declaration of Independence, Mr. Lincoln said, "gave liberty, not alone to the people of this country, but, to the world for all future time."

She raised her eyes. There was nothing more to read. Pressing her thumb and forefinger together, she smiled, then picked up the apple and ate it slowly. Finishing it, she tossed the seeds to a hen pecking nearby and put the core in her pocket for the pig. She reached for the pencil that had lain in her lap and flattened the book so she could write in it.

> *"April, 1886,"* she wrote, her fingers closing tightly around the pencil to keep them steady. "I am advised the General Assembly of the State of Connecticut, at their January Session, have voted me an annual pension for the rest of my life. This will mean for me comfort and security, even a little dignity. The petition bore one hundred and twelve names, many of them familiar to me as sons and grandsons of men I once knew in Canterbury. The first name and the chief promoter is that of Thomas G. Clarke, Andrew Judson's nephew. Now, in these pages, I must write the words of the document which I have committed to memory—
>
> > To the Honorable, the Senate and House of Representatives, in General Assembly convened; We, the Undersigned, Citizens of this State, and of the Town of Canterbury, mindful of the dark blot that rests upon our fair fame and name, for the cruel outrages

inflicted upon a former citizen of our Commonwealth, a noble Christian Woman (Miss Prudence Crandall, now Mrs. Philleo) at present in straightened circumstances, and far advanced in years, respectfully pray your Honorable Body to make such late reparation for the wrong done her, as your united wisdom, your love of justice, and an honorable pride in the good name of our noble State, shall dictate.

It will be remembered that she stands in the Records of the Court as a convicted criminal for the offense of teaching colored girls to read, and suffered unnumbered outrages in person and property, for a benevolent work that now, to its great honor, the General Government itself is engaged in.

We respectfully suggest that you make a fair appropriation in her behalf, which shall at once relieve her from any anxiety for the future, and from the official stigma that rests upon her name, and purge our own record from its last remaining stain, in connection with the colored race.

And your Petitioners will ever pray.

She lifted her head. Often during the past years the plains' wind had swept around her and in it she had heard the pealing of bells that marked some significant triumph. She had not thought to hear the bells peal for her.

"Thank you, oh dear people of Connecticut," she murmured, "I wonder if you know how happy you have made me."

Hearing the sound of children's voices in the house, she picked up her flat-crowned hat and prepared to go in. Another moment and the sun would have gone, leaving the broad plains shadowless. Looking toward the light, she moved her fingers as if to close them around the hand of someone near her.

"This, too, can be a beginning," she said, then turned and went into the house.